Eyes *in the* Mirror

Eyes *in the* Mirror

JULIA MAYER

sourcebooks
fire

Published by Sourcebooks Fire, an imprint of Sourcebooks, Inc.

P.O. Box 4410, Naperville, Illinois 60567-4410

(630) 961-3900

Fax: (630) 961-2168

teenfire.sourcebooks.com

Library of Congress Cataloging-in-Publication data is on file with the publisher.

Printed and bound in the United States of America.

VP 10 9 8 7 6 5 4 3 2 1

To Mom, Dad, and Jesse,
for always answering the phone

3 5 4 9 ~ ~

7

2 4 25 34 22 11

2 8 13 15 16 36

29

7   4 36 37   26
   12   40

chapter 1

A Feeling of Light

Samara

I couldn't stop staring at the razor on the rim of my bathtub.
It was bright pink and sparkly. The handle was soft, and the
blades were contoured to avoid cutting my legs when I shaved.
And now, that was all I wanted from it.

I picked it up and turned it over in my hands. I looked at my
hand, my wrist, my arm. I ran my left hand over my right arm,
touched my cheek to my shoulder, and looked down. My shoulder
felt so soft, and my arms were so smooth and clean. They needed
cuts. I needed to ruin this. I needed to feel something, anything.

Suddenly, I was very aware of the tension in my shoulders, my
clenched back, and my curled toes. I put the razor against my
skin, just under my left shoulder, and I pulled it straight across.
I saw the three horizontal slashes. I watched the blood run down
my arm. The cuts were shallow.

I would get better at this over time. I would learn to break the
razors I bought so that I could hold each blade individually and
make deeper cuts. I felt the pressure drain out of me as I ran
water over a washcloth. I used the washcloth to blot the drip-
ping blood and clean myself up and then soaked the cloth until
it looked clean.

It was just like my health teacher had said it would be. I had listened to her put down all of my other vices. She had told me that there was no such thing as safe sex, that marijuana was a gateway drug, and that if I smoked I would die within four years. And then I'd listened to her tell me not to cut myself.

I used to squirm when I heard people talk about cutting. Taking a razor to your own flesh never seemed logical to me. But in reality, it's wonderful. You can cut into yourself all the frustrations people take out on you.

All the pieces of my life started to come back together after that. My dad was happy with me again. He saw his sweet little girl coming back, the one who'd disappeared after Mom died. I was happy with myself because everyone else thought I was fine. They thought I was learning how to cope, how to live, how to be happy, and only I knew the truth. And knowing the truth gave me power over all of them.

Every cut, every welt, every scar was my revenge on the world for making me who I was, for all of the wrong paths they sent me down, for all of the bad things they had made me do. The cuts were revenge on my dad for everything he had put me through. And on my mom for leaving me. These scars were mine alone, and nobody could take them away.

∽

I didn't do it because of my father's girlfriends, or "lady friends" as he called them. Though having them around the house certainly didn't help. They were everything I expected them to be. Based on this selection, I don't know how he wound up with my mom in the first place. The women he brought home were horrible. They were mean or patronizing or young or old or just…strange.

Immediately after meeting me, one of them acquired the habit of walking away in the middle of my sentences. She would ask me a question and then just as I was responding, she would leave. And she was one of my favorites. At least she didn't pretend to try to befriend me. It was easier being invisible.

Another one was frightened of elevators. My dad had suggested we could all go out for dinner together so we could get to know each other, and I ran into her in the lobby of his office building. She was closer to the call button but didn't use it. Instead she stared straight ahead.

We stood there for a moment until I realized that she wasn't going to catch on to the problem. So I leaned over and pushed the call button. The elevator doors opened and I would have walked in, but she continued standing there, blocking the entrance. I don't know if she was expecting a magic-carpet ride into the elevator, but she refused to move in. So I suggested we take the stairs.

"What's the matter with the elevator?" she asked, scurrying up the stairs behind me. At least my father's office was only on the fourth floor.

My father wasn't purposely ignoring my feelings; he just didn't really give any thought to what sort of effect his dating would have on me.

It took at least half a dozen of these women before he found someone that even I couldn't hate. Caroline. She was sweetness personified, the first to care about how I felt about her appearance in my life. I wanted so much to hate everything about her, just like I hated the others, but she made it impossible. And no matter how hard I tried, I couldn't keep my vow not to like her. I opened up and let her in. I should have known that could only end in her leaving.

It wasn't a car crash, a horrible accident, or any sort of vicious death. It was just me…being me. Caroline realized how hard watching my father date was for me. "Talk to him, Samara. He cares about you. He just doesn't know how to show it. Help him," she told me. So I did. Dad and I were doing the dishes together one night—just the two of us.

"Dad?"

"What can I do for you, Pumpkin?"

"Can we talk?" I let a plate with soggy bits of rice on it clink in the sink. "I…I'm having some trouble accepting that you date." I held my breath, and then a haze seemed to wash over my mind. The rest of the words tumbled out in a fast stream. "I thought Mom was the only woman you could ever love, and now you've forgotten about her and you bring home these horrible women who don't even care about you and they're so mean to me. I don't understand how you could just forget."

My father stood staring, stunned, with a half-dry glass in his hand. His mouth hung open and his eyes seemed unnaturally wide. Then he silently took my hand, still soapy with dish suds, and led me upstairs to my room. He opened my closet door and stood me in front of the full-length mirror.

"Look at you. I could never forget your mother."

I shook my head angrily, choking back tears. "I'm not Mom."

"I know that, but you have her in you. In your eyes and chin, of course, but also in your heart and mind. That's how I can keep living without being afraid of forgetting." He turned me so that I faced him. "But I wish I had known you were so upset. You can tell me anything. You know that, don't you? It can be just the two of us for a while."

The next day he broke up with Caroline. I could picture her in the restaurant, shocked, sad, and disappointed.

I hadn't meant for him to do that. I tried to tell him, but he insisted it was "right for us." So, Caroline's disappearance was my fault. I'm not to blame for my mother's death. I'm not to blame for Ms. Herwitz's disappearance. Caroline was my fault, though. And I'll never forget that. I can imagine what she would say if she knew what had happened. If she knew it was my fault their relationship ended.

"I cared about you enough to connect and to help you connect with your father. And now this?" she would say. And she would be right. Was this how I repaid her? She was one of the only people who had tried to reach out to me. And in retrospect, after this, well, it didn't surprise me at all that so few people had tried.

It was around that time that I started to need cutting instead of wanting it. I broke a new razor, storing the handle in the dresser in my room with all the others that I had saved for no reason, grabbed one of the blades, and lashed into myself. I made four deep cuts at the top of each leg and allowed the blood to drip onto the white tile floor of the bathroom. I sat down and waited, and when most of it had dried, I washed up, washed the floor, and went to bed.

I tried to silence myself after Caroline left. I tried to quiet my mind and watch others be happy. I thought maybe if I could see how they were happy, I would understand how to be happy and I could be happy myself. I had always been happy when I had no one. It was when I opened up to someone that I got hurt. Every time.

~

My birthday was five months later, right before school started. My dad and I spent it together, just the two of us. A month later I met Ms. Herwitz, who would have been the best birthday present ever. Everyone has one of them: that incredible person who makes you rethink your entire life until that point and reshapes everything that comes after.

She had an annoying bubbly happiness that only comes from the kind of adult who had a perfect Disney-movie childhood. She was trim and fit. There was a kind of beauty about her that reeked of perfection. She seemed to have such an overwhelming belief that she was beautiful that you almost had to believe it yourself, even though she never seemed vain or self-obsessed. It's hard to describe—a glow, I guess. A lot like the glow my mother used to have. Or I thought she had.

Ms. Herwitz's first day in class concluded with a conversation about the meaning of life. For all I remember, we could have been talking about the Monty Python movie—she was just a substitute; she had no bearing on our grades or anything so we were all just talking. One of the boys in my class said he thought his life was meaningless, and the conversation warped into something serious.

"Well, I think it's sometimes true that a life can have no meaning," said Ms. Herwitz. "But it's really up to you." She paused, and for some reason she chose to look right at me. "There is always another bad person. Another person who is evil and who hates and scapegoats. But there's only one good person. Only one person who stands up for what is right. There is a group of bad people, and there are an infinite number of people to replace the leader. But a good person is one of a kind. So be a good person and be one of a kind or be one cruel person of many. It's up to you."

When I got to school on Thursday, Ms. Herwitz was gone. My old teacher was back, and nobody seemed to really remember that Ms. Herwitz had even been there. I had just started to get to know her. I had spoken to her Wednesday afternoon; I'd specifically waited until everyone had filed out of the classroom and it was just the two of us. She'd stood, leaning back with her arms on the edge of her desk, still looking summery in her long, open, flowered shirt and black skirt.

"Ms. Herwitz, I want to talk to you about the piece we wrote in class yesterday," I said. "You know, the one about what we'd do if we could have any job in the world?" I had written about designing clothes. I used to do that with my mom when I was little, and it reminded me of her.

Ms. Herwitz nodded, smiling and looking me in the eye. "I was hoping you would talk to me about that, Samara. Your writing is good, but you have to get out of your regular realm of thinking when you write for me. I want to see *you* in your writing. I want to see the person you hide from everyone, even yourself. This kind of writing is where you should let *you* come out."

The look of confusion and frustration on my face didn't stop her, but her smile softened. In that moment, her resemblance to my mother was uncanny.

"Nobody has one self," she continued. "Most people have two, but my sense is that you have three. There is the self you present to the world and the person nobody ever meets. Everyone has those. But you have something more, something you see when you look in the mirror, something you're afraid of. The mirror sees something totally different. Let that person out. All the time, or if not all the time, then at least sometimes. At least in your writing."

All I had wanted to do was discuss my paper. But what she said started the dominoes falling, even though I didn't know it at the time—falling toward what eventually helped me accept the truth of the discovery. It reminded me of a similar conversation I'd had with my mother so many years before, right before she died.

"Baby love, be yourself as much as you can, but be someone else as much as you need to be. Your true feelings are more important than anything. But sometimes, to get to share your true feelings, you have to hide them first. It means sometimes you're going to have to cry when nobody's looking so you can smile when they are. If you have to be someone else for a little while so you can be yourself for a long while, it's okay. But don't get so wrapped up in the person you're pretending to be that you forget who you are."

And now here was this woman telling me exactly what my mother had, but in different words. I had been avoiding thinking about the advice my mother gave me. It was too hard because I knew it was how she'd spent her whole life—pretending to be happy. But Ms. Herwitz forced me to think of it again.

Then she did exactly what my mother had. She left, without so much as saying good-bye. Except instead of dying, she disappeared without a trace.

Nobody said a word about her on Thursday. When I asked other kids where Ms. Herwitz had gone, they shot each other deep glances that I couldn't interpret. It was like being in an episode of *The Twilight Zone*, except it wasn't strange. Not at the time. The disappearance just reinforced the facts: everyone I care about vanishes from my life. It seemed logical that Ms. Herwitz was the next to follow.

That day, a new distraction came into my life. I was so sure that I would be able to get through high school as a loner. I didn't think I needed anything more than my room and my thoughts.

I wasn't sure why anyone would try to be friends with me after all of the reclusive signals I sent, but Dee was always a better person than I was. It was the first time I had noticed her, but the school was huge and that didn't seem that unusual to me. What was weird, though, was that she just came up and started talking to me.

Even a month after school started, it was still warm enough that I could sit outside and eat alone instead of in the cafeteria. But here was somebody interrupting my solitude. She didn't give me a choice; she stood in front of me, hands on hips, and started talking.

"Hi, I'm Dee. I don't think we've met. I noticed that you were sitting over here under the best tree in the place, and I don't think you get to hog all the great space. I just moved into the neighborhood so today is my first day at school here. What about you? Did you grow up here?"

I glared at her. She was beautiful. She had coffee-colored skin and big, bright pink lips, and she smelled like the rain forest. Her hair was wavy and full. She was wearing a black T-shirt with a short sweater over it, a floral miniskirt, and dark tights. Her boots reached to just below the lacy end of her tights. And with one hand on her hip, talking to me, she looked like a doll. Just the way I'd dreamt of looking.

If I were prettier than I am, had more confidence than I do, and had better posture and nicer clothes, I would look exactly like Dee. I wondered why she would want to talk to me anyway. I continued staring at her, wondering if she would just go away.

Instead, she sat down next to me, stretching her legs out and putting her right leg over her left. She leaned back on her hands and shook her hair out behind her. Her hair caught the light, showing her natural highlights.

Dee had this way of turning every positive up ten notches and every negative into a positive. She was happy and bright and cheerful all the time. For one day, Dee was more than a friend to me. She was like the perfect reflection. The person I so desperately wanted to be but couldn't quite manage to become.

She took a deep breath and turned to me smiling. "How do you feel about mechanical soldiers?" she asked.

"What?" Who was this girl, and what kind of question was that? "I don't know. I guess I've never thought about them."

"So pick a side," she said. "You'll probably prove my point and I'll probably prove yours, but who cares? It's true with everything. Even if you don't believe what you think you believe, at least you know what you think by the end."

"I know what I think."

"So what do you think of mechanical soldiers?"

It was a ridiculous question. But what Dee said stuck with me. She dropped a ton of little tips like that. Things that were important but that she didn't even seem to think about. Like how to argue yourself into an opinion: she even convinced me that ice cream was health food later that day. I understood Dee, and she was able to give me so much. She gave me a feeling of light, a feeling I hadn't had in years.

My last class that day was gym, and I decided to cut it to hang out with Dee. She suggested that we go ice-skating at an indoor place nearby. She, of course, was perfectly dressed for it in her little skirt and sweater, whereas in my sweatpants and heavy long-sleeved shirt I was not prepared for ice-skating at all, so instead we went for a long walk and wound up at a coffee shop.

We sat for a little bit and just watched people walking by. But it was starting to get dark and I needed to get home. As much fun as I was having, I still needed time to…stress release (that was how I had started thinking of it) and clean up before my dad came home. Dee said she was going to grab another coffee, but she popped up to give me a hug before I left.

I was halfway down the block when I realized that I had grabbed Dee's bag of scones instead of my own bag of cookies. I ran back to switch but didn't see her anywhere in the café. I asked the barista if she had seen the girl I was with leave.

"Yeah, she went in there," she said, pointing toward the bathrooms and popping her gum loudly.

I walked into the bathroom just in time to see the end of Dee's boot disappearing into the mirror. And then there she was, standing in the mirror staring at me. I looked around the empty bathroom. Then I looked at my reflection showing me pasty white—with my mouth agape. I blinked and looked again and all of a sudden it was Dee's image standing in the mirror staring at me. It would be impossible to say which of us looked more shocked.

chapter 2

It All Began

Dee

My friend Jamie brought me to the party where it all began. It was right after junior year started. We were in some guy's basement. It opened into his backyard, but the door was closed to keep the smoke in the room and it was working. Jamie always invited me to these parties even though he knew I didn't smoke. I appreciated it. I always like to say it's not that I don't do anything; it's just that I'm not doing it tonight.

I was listening to a dull conversation about all the times the people next to me had gotten high before and thinking about leaving. I let my mind wander over the room. The ceiling was that stucco stuff with little sparkles in it. I've wondered how they make those stick to the ceiling. I couldn't even get glitter to stick to the kitchen floor when I tried painting it when I was six. (It seemed like a good idea at the time.)

The house was cookie-cutter—like all the other ones on the block—and even though I know a lot of people don't like houses and neighborhoods like that, there was something comforting about being able to walk into any of my friends' houses and predict exactly which direction the basement would be in and which of two rooms they would occupy. And it was equally comforting to know that my family, my mom and I, are not like this. Nothing about our life is cookie-cutter. When Jamie and I had arrived to help set up, there had been a couple of big, comfy inflatable chairs around. My favorite one had a matching inflatable pillow and footrest, but over the course of the three or four hours since then, most of the chairs had been deflated to make room for more people. I was stuck standing now. I'd given up my chair to get a soda at some point, and by the time I came back, it was gone, moved somewhere probably. After all, there are some benefits of furniture filled with air.

My feet were starting to hurt and the air was getting heavier with smoke, so I was just about to get my stuff and get going when Jamie caught my eye and gestured that I should come over. I did, and chairs being the commodity that they were, Jamie pulled me sideways onto his lap. He was talking with three other people about God, the universe, and the idea of other intelligent life. I wondered if this conversation would be more interesting if I was stoned, and I thought that if I waited another half hour or so, I'd probably wind up with a contact high and I could find out.

Jamie took a hit off the bowl that was coming around. Even though he was dressed for a party like everyone else, he just looked more put together than the other guys there. I guess I always think that about him. It might be because his hair is always buzzed so it never looks messy. Plus it's really fun to touch the back of a guy's neck after he's had his hair buzzed. I resisted the urge to do that while Jamie pulled me backward so that he could reach over me and hand the bowl to the girl next to me.

"You skipped your girlfriend," she said, rolling her eyes and passing it back to me.

"Oh, no. I'm anemic..." I trailed off and Jamie laughed at me.

"Anemic? What does your iron level have to do with it?"

I shrugged sheepishly. It had seemed like a good explanation.

He smiled and looked back at the other girl. "She's not my girlfriend." I saw her perk up. "Take it," he said, still trying to hold his breath in. "I mean," he exhaled in the other direction, "sorry. I just assumed you guys knew each other. This is my friend Dee. Dee," he looked at me, "this is Cassie. She knows Taylor."

Taylor was a friend of Jamie's from school. He and I were in some class or other together, but I couldn't remember which. Cassie was pretty but way overdressed. The rest of us were basically in jeans and T-shirts, and she looked ridiculous to me in her sparkly low-cut tank top.

I shook my head at the bowl and waved it away. I started to move to the arm of the chair Jamie was on, but he tightened his arms around my waist so I stayed put. Cassie shrugged, lit up, and took another hit.

"Anyway," said Taylor, "I think there's an alternate universe. But I think we gotta go all the way out there to find it. We have to break the solar system or something."

I liked the idea of breaking the solar system. I laughed, wondering which part of the solar system would be the easiest to break. Maybe the not-planet Pluto.

"Nah, man. You got it all wrong," Jamie said. "If they ever find another universe, it's gonna be right here under our noses. We're gonna kick ourselves for not seeing it before." It would be a long time until I knew—and even longer until *he* knew—that was a life-changing statement.

"Definitely," Cassie agreed immediately.

I felt Jamie squeeze my hand. What if he was right?

"I think if there's another world it'll look just like this world, but it'll still be crazy different," he said.

I couldn't imagine the solar system just falling apart and leaving people alive and well to witness it, but another universe that you just had to see, just had to be looking for, that was something to work toward, something to hope for. I loved the idea.

My thoughts started racing, and I felt my breathing get really shallow. I was gulping in more smoke than air and I needed to get up, to get someplace else, as quickly as possible. Something incredible was happening, and nobody knew it but me.

I got up to try to steady myself. I went into the bathroom and locked the door, leaning against the sink for support. I stared at myself in the mirror and reminded myself to take deep breaths. I felt like all of a sudden I had the key to a door I hadn't even known existed. I splashed some water on my face and heard somebody pound on the door.

"Just a second," I called.

"Umm, now," the person outside the door called back. I guess taking over the bathroom for 10 or 15 minutes when people are getting drunk isn't the best idea in the world. I took one last deep breath and stared at my paint-speckled shirt in the mirror. I ran my hands over my hair, moving a couple of curls out of the way.

Jamie was still talking to Cassie. On the one hand, I didn't want to interrupt them because she obviously liked him. But on the other hand, well, he was the one who had invited me, and it would be rude to leave without saying good-bye.

I loved how restless his hands were when he talked. He was always running his hands over the back of his neck or tapping his fingers. He'd always start by tapping to the music that was on, but eventually he would get too impatient with that and go off on the beat that was in his head.

It was like he was always waiting for something more, something more interesting or new or, I don't know, just something. And whatever else he was doing, his heel was always tapping the floor really lightly. Anyone who didn't already know that about him probably wouldn't notice because the movement was so small. Right now the tapping was a little heavier, and I knew that meant he was restless.

I leaned down at the side of his chair. "I think I'm going to head out."

Jamie looked at me. "It's late. Do you want me to walk you home?"

"No, I can make it. Stay and have fun with your friends. I'll see you in school on Monday." Jamie absentmindedly moved a few strands of my hair out of his way.

"Well, I'll just walk you out then." Then to Cassie, "I'll catch up with you later."

"Did you have a good time?" he asked me on our way up the stairs.

17

"Very good. Mostly because of you. You gave me a lot to think about."

"Really?" he asked. "I didn't think it was possible to have a thought you hadn't had first."

I felt myself get red, and I was glad we were outside and it was dark. "Don't say that. You know you're smart," I said, touching his arm. Walking me out became walking me to the end of the block, but from there I insisted on walking home myself. I don't like girls who can't walk six blocks alone, especially in a neighborhood like mine that's completely safe.

When I told Jamie that, he smiled a little bit and said, "Okay, get home safe then. Let me know when you're home?"

"I will." I gave Jamie a quick hug.

Jamie and I had known each other for a long time. We had been on-and-off friends since our elementary schools had merged into one middle school. Our sixth-grade social studies teacher had put us next to each other. We used to trade candy because Jamie always brought little bags but he didn't like the red ones—and the red ones were my favorite. But something had been different lately. I couldn't quite wrap my head around it yet, but there was definitely something new with us.

Maybe that's why I took his suggestion of an alternate universe so seriously. If there was an alternate universe, where was it? Who would be there? Anyone different, anyone new? It must be what artists tapped into every time they created something. But I wanted more than that. I wanted a universe I could touch and be a part of it.

But there was a flaw, of course. Where could this alternate universe be? If it was right under my nose and I had been looking for it the whole time, why hadn't I found it?

As I put the key into the front door of my building, I wondered for a moment if Jamie had gone back inside to talk to Cassie. I didn't think so; he had looked pretty bored when he was talking to her earlier. And he had come outside with me, probably just to get away from her.

I walked up to the third floor and down the hall. I stood outside the apartment door for a moment. For some reason, I wasn't ready for this night to be over. There were too many more things to think about. I leaned my back against the wall and heard my phone beep.

I took it out of my jeans pocket and flipped it open. There was a text from Jamie. "Home safe? Didn't stumble into an alt univ on your way? Better bring me back something if you did. ;)"

I smiled to myself, texted him I was fine, and went inside.

I stuck my head into my mom's room. She was sleeping and I hated to wake her, but I knew if I didn't she would be worried in the morning.

"Mom?" I whispered. "Mom?"

I heard her roll over. "You have a good time, honey?"

"Yeah, I did. Thanks. Sorry to wake you."

"That's okay. I sleep better knowing you're here safe anyway." I heard her move around under the blankets and walked over toward her, my eyes starting to adjust to the darkness. I leaned down and kissed her forehead.

"Sleep well."

"You too," she said, and I could tell she was already drifting back to sleep.

～

The unfortunate thing about junior year is that it doesn't give you much time to go looking for entrances to an alternate universe. I had always been a good student, but with college applications coming up the next year, my grades were especially important. Plus I didn't want to get to the point where I was looking so hard that I just made something up. I wanted to find something that really existed.

A few weeks later, there was a really muggy day and I wanted to get into cool bathwater instead of waiting until the next morning to shower. I looked at myself in the mirror and noticed my shirt. My mom and I had decided to paint the entire apartment one weekend. We only got as far as the living room and kitchen before we gave up. Painting isn't as easy as it looks. Due to a combination of drips and a small paint fight, most of the paint wound up on us and my plain, green shirt had gotten speckled with red and baby blue.

It was my favorite shirt, and I'd worn it to the party with Jamie. As I looked at it on the bathroom floor, I thought back to the fifteen minutes I had spent in the bathroom at the party that night. I began to think about the alternate universe Jamie had suggested. Something better than my own world, something that seemed just like this world but was actually completely different.

I used my right hand to readjust my towel around my left

shoulder as I sat next to the tub, waiting for it to fill, and I saw my reflection use her left hand to touch her right shoulder. I paused for a moment, absentmindedly running my hand over my skin.

I watched my reflection in the water making all the same motions that I did, but the exact opposite. I stared at her for a moment. I thought of Jamie. "It'll look just like this world, but completely different," he had said. I rubbed my cheek against my shoulder, and my reflection made all the same motions I did, but the exact opposite every time. She was exactly what Jamie had said she would be: something identical and completely different at the same time.

I stared at my reflection in the water and began to wonder... I took a deep breath and plunged my head into the cool water. I thought for a moment that I had gotten through and I opened my eyes to look around, but all I got was soap in my eye. It burned.

∾

The bathwater didn't discourage me, though. The mirror seemed like such a perfect place for this alternate universe. Walking to school two days later, I passed my reflection in a store window. I walked toward it, watching my reflection walk toward me. I tapped on the glass. Someone tapped back.

For a moment I thought I had found it. I thought my reflection was there ready to talk to me, tapping back, ready to let me into her world. All I needed to do was know it was there, there was my...I looked past my reflection for a moment and noticed a guy cleaning the inside of the window. He was staring at me, snickering. He waved. I smiled but I felt my shoulders slump. I smiled a little more to try to make it seem like I wasn't crazy.

I became fascinated with mirrors. I'm sure everyone must have thought I was just enchanted with myself. I carried around a hand mirror and checked the mirrors in my locker and the school bathroom all the time. Of course, I couldn't be sure that the alternate universe was in the mirror, but I had a gut instinct. The way you know when you're walking down the street if the person behind you shouldn't be there.

I knew the alternate universe had to be related to the face in the mirror. My face, but not really mine because I have a birthmark on my right cheek and she has one on her left. After I realized this, I could have sworn that once in a while, I would see my reflection fall a half second behind me, but I was sure that was just my imagination. I wanted it to happen so badly that I was pretending to see it, even if it wasn't there.

A week later, I got home from school and stood in front of the full-length mirror in my closet. I tried opening the door and standing behind it. I tried standing in the closet in the dark. I stared at the mirror. "Abracadabra, open sesame," I said to my reflection. I stood back and looked her directly in the eye, saying, "I'd like to get in, please. Open the door and make way for Dee. I'm ready to come in and I want to meet you, so open up." I thought I saw my reflection twitch, but no door opened. None of the words made any difference.

The girl in the mirror was exactly who I wanted to meet, someone who lived in a world like mine but was still just the opposite, but it wasn't until my mom got involved that I had any sort of breakthrough.

She was worried about me. I guess she, of all people, couldn't believe I was vain enough to be looking at myself all day, but she also couldn't understand what I was looking at besides my own reflection. I came home from school the day after I'd tried all the magic words to find her taking down the mirror in my room.

"Mom, my mirror!" I screeched.

"Sweetheart, I'm concerned about what you're seeing in this thing. It's a distraction to you. I don't want you getting involved in this…in this staring at yourself all the time." She said it calmly, and hard as I tried, I couldn't argue her out of her decision. She held the top of the mirror firmly, and I grabbed the bottom. As though I would ever overpower my mom. We must have pulled and let go at the same time because the mirror fell and broke at the same moment that my mom lost her balance and fell into the shards on the floor, disappearing to the other side of the mirror.

I saw it in slow motion, but it happened so fast. For a second, it looked like she was going to fall and cut herself on the glass. But rather than getting cut, her hand went straight through the floor, and then her arm. It was like when you see a car accident happening, but you're a block away and there's nothing you can do to stop it.

She just kept falling, and every time I reached for her, she seemed to slip through my fingers. Ghostlike. Disappearing into my floor. *Into my floor?* How can someone just disappear into a floor, into shards of glass on the floor?

For a moment I thought I would be able to grab her leg, but just as I reached for it, she was gone. Gone into the mirror. Into the shards of a mirror that was broken on my floor. Into the world that I hadn't even really believed existed. But there had to be something. There was no other explanation.

She should have just fallen and gotten scratched up. Her hands should have bled, and maybe her pants should have gotten cut up. But instead, she just kept falling. Falling past everything into something. Or into nothing.

I stared after her, looking at the empty hands I had thought were holding on to her. What had just happened? I was speechless, terrified, alone, petrified, horrified. I had made my mother disappear, the one person I loved most in the entire world. The one person I could trust, the one person who knew what to do when terrible things happened. I stared at my colorless face in the shards of glass on my floor.

My mom is usually the person I go to when I don't know what to do. She's the one who fixes things when I mess them up. She's the one who…just disappeared. People don't just disappear. They don't just fall through floors or into mirrors or into other worlds. How would you get them out if they did? Where was my mother? What the hell had just happened? There was only one person who, maybe, might believe me.

∾

I ran to his house and knocked on the door. Jamie answered and looked at me just a little bit wide-eyed.

"Dee, what's wrong? You look…Are you okay? Come in. Sit down."

I tried to catch my breath as I sat down and started talking. "I'm…Well, I think…I don't know. I'm not sure."

Then I blurted out the whole story. I was terrified he was going to think I was crazy. *I* thought I was crazy. But I had just seen it; it had just happened a minute ago. But I still couldn't believe it. When I got to the part about trying to find the door, he whistled quietly, "I don't think anybody has ever taken me that seriously, let alone when I'm stoned."

"Focus! My mom is missing!"

"Okay, so what do we need to do? How do we get her back out?" he asked, popping up and beginning to pace back and forth across the living room.

"I think I have to go in after her. I mean, now that I know how, I don't think there's any other way to get her out."

"Do you really think that's a good idea? I mean, what if it doesn't work? What if you get stuck, or you get hurt or something? What if you didn't see what you thought you saw? What if…" The what-ifs kept coming. And finally they ended with, "Why don't…why don't I go with you?"

I looked at him. "Oh, no. You don't have to get involved. This is my thing. I just wanted advice, and I needed someone to talk to."

"I want to go with you," he said, sitting down on the couch next to me and rocking back and forth a little bit.

"I really think this might be something I have to do alone. This is the world that I found, and it's my mom I'm trying to get back. I don't know. Plus I think it would help if you could be here to cover for me. Can you come up with a good reason for me to be gone?"

Jamie popped up and started pacing in a circle around the living room again. I loved that he was always moving, never boring. "Well, your mom's a nurse. So you two could be going away to take care of someone. Like your grandma or something."

That made more sense than anything I could have thought of. And the babbling that came out of my mouth was nothing compared to the babbling going on inside my head. There were thousands of what-ifs. What if she was already gone? What if there was no way to bring her back? What if I never saw my mom again?

We called my mother's office and told them she was taking a couple of sick days. I couldn't imagine that getting her back would take more than a couple of days. Provided I was able to find her. I asked Jamie to tell the school the following day that I was with my mom somewhere. I wanted to get going as soon as possible. I was so scared that something might happen to my mom. Jamie walked me toward the door. I stopped him at the front and gave him a hug and a kiss on the cheek.

"Be careful. Just watch out, and come back if it doesn't feel safe. And if it's awesome, well, no matter how much you like it, promise to come back?" he asked.

I nodded and turned to walk back to my apartment. I could

see my feet moving but I felt numb. Something in me had taken over, and my feet were moving me forward without my head giving them any direction.

When I got home, I went into the bathroom, the room with the hardest floor that would make breaking the mirror easiest, and dropped another mirror. I watched the glass shatter and could feel myself pause. I reminded myself that I needed to do this. I took a deep breath and felt even my lungs tremble. I tried to fall into it just the way my mother had, and I guess it was close enough because when I fell, I didn't land on the hard, cold floor covered in broken glass.

I didn't land. At all.

My body trembled. My head swirled. The world disappeared behind me and exploded in front of me at the same time. I forced my eyes open, afraid of what would happen if I closed them.

There were colors I had never seen before. The sun burst open. I was overwhelmed by beauty and light and a complete feeling of awe. I made desperate attempts to feel any part of my body, but my legs seemed to have disappeared. It felt like hours before I could find them. I struggled to stand but couldn't tell which way was up. Which were my arms and which were my legs.

And then all of a sudden, everything was black. And I was there. My body was still. I could be sure again that it existed. That I existed. I was compelled to step forward and almost jumped back as I saw my leg step out of a mirror in front of me and into a school bathroom.

I knew I didn't want to go back, but going forward seemed

terrifying. I couldn't just stand there, so I stepped out and looked around, unsure of what to do and how to react. Why here? What was I doing in a high-school bathroom, and who was the reflection looking back at me? I touched the mirror and my hand went right through it, like I was touching a pool of water. This was what I had wanted when I'd touched the water in the bathtub the first time.

I wanted to run out of the bathroom and race down the hallway looking for my mother, but I heard people coming. I didn't know how they would react to me, so I locked myself in a stall. Would they look like me? Would they recognize me as an outsider? Would they ask what I was doing here?

One of them leaned into the mirror, and I worried that she was going to fall straight through. But the mirror was solid and she applied lipstick fine.

"Do you think this color is too orange for my skin tone?" she asked one of her friends.

Her friend cocked her head to one side and squinted. "No. I think it's pretty. I mean, not for me. But definitely for you." They nodded to each other. I heard one of them wash her hands, and they left the bathroom.

I was so disappointed. After all of this work, the people were just the same as the people I had left. They were the same makeup- and boy-obsessed girls I had left behind. I couldn't focus on that, though. I had to find the people I was looking for. Where was my mother? Was she okay? Where was my reflection—the girl I kept seeing in the mirror?

I walked out of the bathroom and looked down the hall. I found my mother immediately and tried to wave, but she didn't see me. I went over and said hello, and she looked at me but didn't seem to recognize me.

"It's…it's me. Umm, do you want to…"

She looked at me, and I thought it was her. I thought she was seeing me, her daughter. But she wouldn't say it. She just leaned forward in that sympathetic way adults do when a little kid comes over and says something completely ridiculous.

"Mom?"

She looked at me that same way for another minute before seeming to decide I was okay. "I'm…I'm sorry. I'm just a substitute."

"But…no. You're not just a substitute. You're the real thing. You're…" But I couldn't bear to say it again. I was afraid I might burst into tears if I did. "I guess, umm, okay," I said and began to turn around.

I saw her walk away quickly out of the corner of my eye, and just as I thought I was about to lose it, something else caught my attention. There she was. My reflection.

It took me another day to figure out that my mother was teaching in this world and another two days to figure out how to get her out and back into the world where she belonged. After the first time, I couldn't talk to her. It upset me too much to think that my mother didn't know me. I needed her help. I needed her to comfort me and care that I was upset. I would walk up to her and be just another student. Just another kid in school. Except a stranger, because I didn't have classes with her. Well, I didn't have classes at all.

I spent a few days wandering the school, going back home through the mirror to sleep at night and returning in the morning. After the first time, the sensation was never as intense. I was just walking from one world into the other, like walking through a door. A dark door.

I switched between following my reflection around and following my mother around. Within the first hour of arriving, I wasn't sure which one was more important to me. The two talked a lot, which made it a little bit easier. I could watch them together without having to run back and forth all the time.

A few times I tried to get close enough to hear them, but I was concerned about them seeing me. I wasn't sure how I would explain myself. I wasn't even really sure they could see me. I thought they could, but it was confusing and I didn't want to make the situation worse by making this woman who didn't know that she was my mom not trust me and not want to come back with me.

On Thursday morning, I saw my mom, or the woman who was usually my mom, walk into the faculty bathroom. I knew it could be my one shot. I followed her in there as quietly as I could and hid in one of the stalls. I watched her walk out of a stall through the crack in the door. She had been wearing variations on the same outfit for three days, and I wondered, not for the first time, where she had been sleeping. The clip-clop of her shoes across the floor stopped, and she smoothed her skirt and turned the water on.

I prayed silently that what I was about to do would work, that I wouldn't wind up with the woman in front of me having a big bruise on her head instead of finding my mother on the other side of the mirror with me.

I unlocked the door and pushed it open while she was looking down and washing her hands. Before she could look up and figure out what was happening, I ran up behind her, put my arms around her, and ran straight through the mirror, holding on and toppling out over her on the other side.

I stood up, and my mom looked at me confused. What if this was just some woman who looked like my mom? "Mom? It's you, right?"

"Of course it's me. Who else would it be? Are you okay? What just happened?"

She recognized me! "I'm fine. I think you were trying to get something from the top shelf and…" I had a brainstorm. "You've had a fever the last couple of days. You've been really confused.

"When I saw you up here, I just knew you were going to fall, so I came in to try to get you before you did. But you slipped and we fell. I'm sorry. I shouldn't have let you get up. I think the better question is are *you* okay? Does your head hurt?"

"Oh. Well. Yes, I think I'm okay. I feel a little bit…strange. I must have been having some strange dreams. But I'm sure it's nothing."

She had no recollection of what had happened. Or maybe she did, but she thought it was feverish hallucinations. I thought that made more sense than any other explanation I might have been able to come up with. I wasn't going to push her to think about it in any more depth than she already was. I certainly didn't want her to figure out that she had been spending her days in an alternate universe.

∽

I went back to my reflection's school the next day and looked for her at lunch. With my mom back home where she belonged, I could focus all of my attention on my reflection. I wanted to find out whatever I could about her. She was sitting under a tree eating her lunch, lost in thought. This was my moment. I sat down next to her.

"Hi, I'm Dee. I don't think we've met. I noticed that you were sitting over here under the best tree in the place, and I don't think you get to hog all the great space. I just moved into the neighborhood so today is my first day at school here. What about you? Did you grow up here?"

"You're new?" she asked, glaring at me.

Was I? It was the first time we'd met, but we'd actually been spending hours a day together since we were born without knowing it. From her perspective, I supposed I was new, though. I had been haunting the school for a few days now, so I wasn't exactly new to the school. "New to you," I finally settled on.

We talked for two hours. She must have missed at least one class, and I hoped she would be willing to miss another one to hang out with me for the afternoon. I invited her to go ice-skating with me after school that day. There were signs all over saying that a new indoor rink had just opened and that the hockey team would be playing there.

"Just the two of us, once you agree to come," I said, and I saw her smile for the first time.

But she said no. She said she wasn't properly dressed for it. "Besides," she said, "the best part of ice-skating is watching the Zamboni anyway."

"Why?" I asked her.

"I used to want to be the guy who drives the Zamboni. My mom thought that was a great idea. My dad thought it was a bad goal for me to have. He wants me to do something, I don't know…bigger, I guess. But my mom thought it was great. She said they always need Zamboni drivers.

"Those things are so powerful, and the ice looks so clean after they're done. It wipes away all the scars from people's skates." She paused. "And leaves the ice clean and new. Like nothing had ever cut into it at all."

I smiled. I can't think of a kid I know who *didn't* want to be a Zamboni driver at one time or another.

∽

I started to explain to Samara who I really was at least twice that day. "Samara," I said, "I want to explain something to you. I think you need to know something about me." But while I was pausing for a deep breath, I would see her looking at me with her big innocent eyes and I wasn't be able to finish. I chickened out and said something like, "When I was little, my room was separated from the living room by a shower curtain with ducks on it." And she smiled and said, "Good to know."

I was afraid the whole thing would scare her; it scared *me*. So

I left her believing we were just really good friends. Instant best friends, the kind you would give half your Popsicle to when you were a kid. I figured I would wait until the right time and tell her then that I was actually her reflection.

All Samara needed was a friend, and I was prepared to be exactly that for her. I wanted to help her through whatever she was going through. She was clearly in pain, even though she never said it.

We spent the afternoon wandering around parks and in and out of stores. At one point we passed a graveyard, and I was a little thrown by how freaked out Samara got.

"Can we speed up?" she asked.

"Sure," I said. "Why?"

"I just…graveyards. They creep me out. I've never been in one, and it makes me think of…I just…I just don't like them."

After that, I thought it was time to go inside for a while. We went into a café to warm up. Eventually, Samara said she had to get home. She asked if I lived in the same direction as her.

"I don't think so," I told her. I told her I was going to get another cup of coffee or something like that before I left for home. She nodded. I waited until she had turned the corner in the other direction before heading for the café's bathroom. There was nobody in there, so the bathroom mirror seemed safe for me to go through. Just as I stepped in, though, I heard someone walk in behind me. I turned around, and there was Samara, standing and staring at me, pale faced, mouth open, eyes wide. I didn't know what to do. I tried to stay as calm as possible.

"Samara, this is going to be really confusing for you, but I'm just going to say it. I'm your reflection, or you're my reflection. I'm not a real person in your world, but I am a real person. I think. I'm as real here as you are there."

Samara looked at me, screamed, and ran out of the bathroom.

"I didn't want you to find out, not like this," I called after her. But the door had already slammed shut.

I had wanted to become friends before I told Samara. I'd wanted her to know that I liked her and that she could trust me. I felt like I needed to be there for her, and I didn't want to lose that opportunity because she was scared of me. Scared of who I was or who I wasn't. I mean, this *was* terrifying. But at least we could be terrified and excited by it together.

I went home that night and began figuring out what to do. I knew I would have to win back Samara's trust. She was going to have to understand why I did what I did and why I hadn't been able to tell her who I was when I'd met her that afternoon. Otherwise, everything would be ruined, and I could never spend time in the mirror. I needed to help Samara. I needed her to talk to me again.

chapter 3

The Final Proof

Samara

There was paint on the walls, and the third layer down under the peeling yellow and gray in the coffeehouse bathroom was the exact same color as the green of Dee's eyes. As she stood staring at me, stumbling over words to try to explain herself in the mirror, all I could see was the peeling paint on the walls, peeling to reveal true colors underneath.

Dee had lied to me. She had betrayed me and completely hidden who she was. I couldn't believe how much I had opened up to this complete stranger in a day. And how could I be surprised when she'd turned out to be nothing? After everything I had been through, I had tried so hard to avoid letting anyone else in. But I couldn't help it. It was the same as with all the boys I had told myself I didn't have to care about. I had let her in despite my best efforts to avoid it.

I had been right all along. I always am. I try to force myself to believe that someone else can care about me, that someone might want to get to know me just because I'm a cool person, just because they think they might like me. I've done it with everyone in my life.

But Dee was just using me, and I didn't even know for what. Usually I at least know what I'm being used for. I didn't know who Dee was, or even *what* she was. I didn't know what she wanted from me, or what in me had told me that it was safe to open up to her and give it to her.

Angry as I was, I could hear a tiny voice in the back of my head begging me to go back and find out the answers to all the questions I had. What was Dee doing here? What was this other world she talked about? Was she real? Had I finally gone as crazy as everyone thought I was?

When I got outside to the parking lot, I felt that voice getting stronger. I wiped the tears from my eyes and stood, unable to decide what to do. I turned in circles a couple of times before finally deciding to go back into the café. I took a deep breath and pushed the door open. I looked in the mirror in front of me, and…nothing. She wasn't waiting for me to come back. She wasn't standing in the mirror. There was just *me* looking back at me. She had just walked away.

I wondered if I had imagined the whole thing. If Dee was just something I had made up on my way to losing my mind, like hearing things or seeing people who didn't exist. I heard someone flush a toilet in one of the stalls. Real, concrete. If Dee existed at all, it was only barely. It wasn't real. She wasn't here; she wasn't in this world. I felt the tears well up again. I ran out of the bathroom and all the way home.

ॐ

I had tried to be open again, tried to let in people, to care. One of them had disappeared without a trace, and the other one had turned out not to be real. I ran up the stairs to my room and slammed the door. I saw the full-length mirror on my closet door in front of me. I slammed that door too, and was left with nothing to do, so I lay there on the floor screaming silently, hearing only the quiet whir of the ceiling fan.

The tears kept coming, faster and stronger than tears had ever come for anyone else in my life. It was like every failed relationship in my life had been leading up to this moment. To this betrayal. This dual betrayal. I pulled myself off the floor and went into the bathroom, automatically grabbing the razor blade I had put underneath the soap dish.

I started cutting my hip—carving would be a better word—and I would have gone all the way down my leg, but watching the blood drip down was enchanting. I couldn't take my eyes off it. The blood, the physical color and smell, calmed me the way a cigarette calms an addict after years of not smoking.

The bathroom was blue and green with white tile, and the red blood was such a necessary addition to this cold, unforgiving room. I could feel Dee calling to me. Telling me to talk to her. But I couldn't. I was tired of being lied to, tired of people taking advantage of me. I wanted to know who and what she was; I wanted to find out about her. But I hated her, and I refused to give in.

I was sitting in the cabinet under the sink with my knees pulled up to my chest, leaning sideways to avoid the drainpipe and staring at the dried blood on the floor when my father knocked on the door. "Samara. Samara, it's almost time for dinner. Are you okay in there?" I took a deep steadying breath.

"I'm fine. I'll be down in a second."

I splashed cool water on my face, avoiding the face staring back at me in the mirror, reapplied mascara, and walked downstairs to eat dinner with my father. It was the only time we would eat together that week. He asked about my day, and I nodded as nonchalantly as I could. I wasn't sure I could make something up that would make it sound like I had had a normal day.

"I have some good news, Pumpkin."

I looked at him, chewing and not really taking in what he was saying.

"I said I have some good news," he repeated.

"Oh?" I mumbled into my spaghetti.

"I was promoted at work. VP of purchasing. It's a big change for us. It means not only college but a master's, if you want it, or an extra year abroad or whatever makes you happy. And without any debt when you finish."

I nodded, chewing slowly and swallowing.

"Congratulations, Dad. That's great! I'm so…Well, that's great."

"Thanks, Sam. There's a downside, though, that I should tell you about. It means a lot more traveling for me. A lot more time out of town. Is that okay with you? I want to be able to spend more time together. But this could be a big difference for us. For you. In our lives."

Time out of town didn't seem like a bad idea to me at that moment at all. Some time alone sounded perfect. Sounded like exactly what I needed.

"Definitely, Dad. Take it. It's great. Congratulations."

He smiled at me from across the table and nodded. I did my best to smile back at him, and we sat in silence, lost in thought for the rest of dinner until I eventually said I needed to get upstairs and finish my homework.

∽

I swore to myself that I wouldn't give in to the curiosity. I wouldn't give in to missing her the way that I did. I wanted to be mad; I wanted to separate myself from everyone, especially the people using me for their own twisted gain. It lasted three days. Then I gave in.

I was lying in bed. I had been awake most of the time since I found out the truth about Dee, or I had at least spent most of the time between nightmares awake. My mother's death, the boys who had left, a father whose main talent was a disappearing act. I know I had told him it was all right, but his promotion was only the latest addition. One more reason for him not to spend time with me. If it wasn't this, it would've been something else he didn't bother asking permission for.

Losing Dee would just be another in a long line of bad dreams. I sat up in bed. I knew I wasn't going to sleep again if I didn't understand what had happened, what Dee had done, or what she wanted from me.

I walked over to the mirror and looked in. I thought I saw her for a moment, but then I was sure it was a figment of my imagination. I sank down to the floor, put my head in my hands, and whispered, "Where are you, Dee? How could you do this to me? I just can't understand." I looked back up into the empty eyes of my reflection and saw another face appear behind mine. I turned around slowly. And there was Dee standing behind me in my room, face streaked with tears.

"I'm so sorry, Samara. I won't lie to you again. I didn't mean to do this. It just happened and then I didn't want to tell you because I thought you wouldn't understand, so I didn't tell you and then..." she trailed off. I tried to control it but I couldn't. I collapsed into sobs. "I never meant to hurt you. I wanted... I wanted you to be the sister I always wished I had. Please, please trust me."

She looked so earnest, standing in my bedroom at 2 a.m., apologizing. I tried to shake my head, tried to back away, but I couldn't. I nodded and fell into her arms, still crying. She stroked my hair for a moment, and I could feel her tears mixing with my own as they fell.

"I promise not to disappear again. I'm not going anywhere, not until I've told you everything you want to know. Not until you tell me it's okay to leave."

I leaned back for a moment and looked at her. "I promise," she told me, "you'll never lose me. Not for as long as you want me here."

We sat there quietly for what felt like ages before I said anything. I wasn't sure what to say. "Talk to me. What's the mirror world? Which of us is the real one? How did you find this? How did you find me? How did you find out about it?" Every question I thought of led to ten more questions I wanted to ask. And Dee started to explain.

She told me about the party she had been at with Jamie, what he had said, and how she had thought about it for ages. "I was bored out of my mind in my world. I needed to meet someone different and exciting and new. Someone with some personality. The people in my school, in my life, are so boring. I wanted to find, umm, find a mirror opposite," she smiled, "to all of that. I'm just lucky it was you."

"How does it work?" I asked her, turning back to the mirror in my closet and tapping it lightly.

"I think that what happens is that I can only come through when you're looking in the mirror. When I'm here and you look in the mirror, you see basically a photograph of yourself. It's a two-dimensional reflection. But when the two of us are both at the mirror, we see each other.

"My mom was able to get through more easily than I was, I think, because her reflection would be your mom and your mom is dead. If she wanted to, I think my mom could get through any time."

I stood up, staring at the tear-streaked girl looking back at me in the mirror. "So this is what I actually look like? It's strange, isn't it? You and I don't look, well, I mean, we look similar, but we don't look exactly the same. But I've never noticed that I don't look like my reflection, I don't think."

Dee had no explanation for that one. I guess I didn't really need one. She and I look similar enough—especially that night when we were wearing matching yellow pajamas with pink moons—but Dee was much prettier than I was, and I wasn't sure how that could work. If she was my reflection, shouldn't we have looked the same?

∾

After that, Dee started going to her own school again. I went to school but I had never liked it, and now that I had conversations with Dee to look forward to, the days trudged by even slower. I started sleeping through classes just to be fully rested when I talked to Dee at night.

We would both change, brush our teeth, and go sit in front of the mirrors in our rooms talking. "Okay, Dee. You've lived in both worlds. Which one is better?"

"Here's the thing about the different worlds," she said. "I don't think one is better than the other necessarily. Except that I've lived in this world all my life so I find it pretty boring. Yours is more interesting. There are all sorts of crazy things happening and new people to meet."

"You just think that because you didn't have to do anything while you were here."

"What do you mean? I had to stalk you!"

I laughed. I supposed that was true. "Of course, stalking your reflection is more interesting than going to classes. And writing bad papers. I mean, come on. If you had to actually live my life, you wouldn't think this world was so great."

"Maybe you're right. But, well…"

"What?"

"Nothing. I mean, not nothing but…another time."

I rolled my eyes. But my limited experience with Dee told me that I would probably find out sooner if I just kept my mouth shut and waited for her to bring it up again.

I changed the subject. "There's nobody in my world like Jamie, though. Nobody suggested a place to look for an alternate universe to me. So your world has at least one thing on mine. You guys figured out the alternate universe. I never would have figured it out if you hadn't come through to find me."

I saw Dee smile for a second, twirling one of her curls around her finger. "That's true. My world does have Jamie. Or, I mean, people like Jamie. You've got good people in your world too, though. What about that teacher you told me about?"

"She was great. But she disappeared on me. It doesn't sound like Jamie is going anywhere."

"No, he's not." Dee's smile flickered again.

⁓

Dee was always asking questions about my dad. My mom too, the one time, but mostly my dad. I guess it was because she doesn't have a dad, she didn't know how little I wanted to talk about him and the parade of bimbos he'd brought home and the allegiance he felt to his job over me.

"Are you close to your dad?"

"No. At least not anymore. We used to be, I guess, before Mom died. But even then I was much closer to her. She's the only person I ever met who was right about everything. Once in a while we would argue, and it was never long after I stomped off that I realized she was right. I used to hide in here after we fought."

"In your room?"

"In my closet. She'd come up eventually and slip a cookie under the door or ask me to meet her downstairs for a walk or to sit on the swings in the backyard. We used to swing together all the time. When I was little, I always thought she was just thin, but I guess 'gaunt' would be a better word. But since she was so small, we could both fit on the tire swing in the backyard. Then we'd spin it around and around.

"Once in a while, instead of spinning we'd pretend we were the Flintstones and try running as far as we could in our wheel car. And she would quietly explain what she had been saying before and she would be right. She just…always knew what to do, I thought. I guess. I mean, she had a dark side, but she tried to keep it away from me.

"I never really got to say good-bye to her when she died. My dad wouldn't let me go to the funeral. I guess he thought I was too young. And now, I just…I just can't. I miss her, though."

Dee looked at me without saying anything for a moment. "Samara, you don't…you don't have to answer this if you don't want to."

"Okay," I said. "What's the question?"

"How did she die?"

It had been a long time since I had talked about how my mom died. Or even talked about her at all. Dad never liked to talk about her. I think it was just too hard. I looked away but I could still feel Dee's eyes on me. I almost told her that I didn't want to talk about it.

We hadn't actually *known* each other for a long time, but we had in a way, and the two of us clicked. We understood each other, and I had never felt that way with someone. I guess I had never had a real best friend before. I wanted Dee to know about my mom. I wanted her to know everything, almost everything, about me. So I took a deep breath, looked up, and looked her in the eye.

"She killed herself. She was upset because she and Dad had an argument. I had never heard them yell like that before. I just left for school without saying anything, and when I came home she was dead."

"Oh, Samara. I…I had no idea. I'm so sorry." She was quiet for a minute. "You know it wasn't your fault, don't you? I mean, it isn't either of your faults. You or your dad. People don't kill themselves over one fight, even a big one. You know that, don't you?"

I nodded. I knew Mom had this other side to her; I had always known. And I had been told that before, but it was good to hear it from Dee too, because I trusted Dee. There was one thing that had always made me feel like it was my fault, though, and I had never told anyone.

"Can I show you something?" I asked Dee. "It's a little scary, but I want to show it to you."

"Of course. What is it?"

I went into my closet, all the way to the back, and found the shirt I had been wearing the day I found my mother. The day she killed herself. I pulled it out. I hadn't looked at in years, but the ink was just as fresh as it had been that day. I called to Dee to come through the mirror so I could show it to her properly, and when I walked back out, she stepped through.

"This is the shirt I was wearing. Look." I pointed to the ink stains. Dee furrowed her eyebrows and stared at the stains.

"It got stained at 1:57 in the afternoon, when my pen broke. It exploded all over me." Dee looked up at me, confused, and I continued. "When I found my mom, the bloodstains on her shirt were in the exact same places. She had taken sleeping pills, but she must have hit her head or something because it was bleeding and there was dried blood all over her shirt. *In exactly these places.* The paramedics said she had probably died between one and three in the afternoon. It was at 1:57, Dee. I know it was."

I had never shown the shirt to anyone, but this was it, the final proof of the connection I had lost when my mom died.

Tears were rolling down Dee's cheeks. She put her arms around me. "I'm so sorry, Samara. I'm—" Her voice cracked and she couldn't say anything else.

I pulled away from her and walked to the far back of my closet to hang the shirt up. I had wanted to throw it away at the time, but I couldn't bring myself to. I knew I could never wear it again. I couldn't even wash it. But for some reason I couldn't let it go either. I felt so much better after telling Dee; something about having someone else know my secret made it easier to keep. I slept well that night.

༒

It was another three days before Dee brought up the suggestion I had let drop. She shocked me, scared me, and entranced me all at the same time. The more I thought about it, the more it seemed like the only natural thing to do.

Switch places, lead each other's lives.

I didn't know why Dee would want to live my life. After all of our time talking, it had become clear that Dee was only becoming more content with her life. She said that was because of the addition of a best friend, and I know she wanted me to think she meant me, but a part of me wondered when she said that if she was talking about Jamie. But she'd suggested it, and I figured if she wanted my crappy life, she could have it.

The only thing that stopped me was that I was afraid of walking through the mirror for the first time. Dee promised it was incredible, and I believed her. But what if I couldn't make it through? What if I wasn't able? If I wasn't good enough? What if I was never able to make it out? Dee swore up and down that would never happen and eventually, whether I believed her or not, my desire to be happy the way she was happy—if only for the day we would switch—overtook me and I agreed. I wanted to be Dee.

I remembered a time, as a little girl, when my mom was still around and I felt happy. That I had trusted people. When spinning on a tire swing was a good way to get out anger instead of carving anger directly into my body. I remembered that time, and I wanted it back. Switching places with Dee would give that to me.

Dee and I agreed: we would switch for one day, two days tops, and we would spend plenty of time talking throughout the day so that we wouldn't mess anything up for each other. It would be incredible.

chapter 4

Breaking the Spell

Dee

There was only one person I knew who would be able to help me get Samara back after she ran out of the bathroom that night.

I pulled him to the side at lunch the next day.

"I found her."

"Your mom?" Jamie asked me.

"No. Well, yes, but she's back and everything is fine. I found my reflection. And she's awesome and interesting and funny and…in pain. And I need to help her. But she found out who I am and she's mad at me and she won't talk to me. What do we do?"

"I don't understand, Dee. I have no idea what to tell you. What does it mean for your reflection to be mad at you? I mean, what do you have to do to make her not mad? Don't you just see her every time you look in the mirror? So I don't know, can't you just talk to her? This alternate world, I know you say it was my idea, but I mean, it's not really. It's yours. It belongs to you. I don't know how to fix it anymore than I understand how you found it."

"Well, can you come over after school and help me figure it out?"

Jamie smiled and agreed he would. We walked back to my house together. He dragged a stick along the fence next to us and jumped up to try to touch the orange fall leaves.

When we got up to my apartment, I sat down on my bed and he sat down on the floor.

"You can take the chair, you know," I said, gesturing to the desk in the corner of my room. When I turned, I noticed that Jamie fit in my room very well.

"I'm fine. I mean, the floor's comfortable. You know, it doesn't really matter where I sit." He smiled a little bit, and the two of us burst into giggles. I threw a pillow at him. He caught it, using it to rest his back against, and asked, "If you just went through and sat her down and tried to talk to her, would she listen? I mean it *is* the easiest solution. It's worth a shot, isn't it? I've listened to you talk. You can convince anyone of anything."

So I tried. But I was only able to get halfway through the mirror. I found myself in a black box between worlds, and I wasn't able to step out the other side. Instead, I was stuck in the middle. It was empty and cold and lonely there, and I went backward as quickly as I could. I wasn't sure what would happen if I walked around the box. I worried that the door back into my own world would close behind me and I would get stuck there.

When I stepped back out, Jamie was sitting on my bed wide-eyed, clutching my teddy bear. "You just disappeared." I smiled at the bear, and he looked down and quickly threw it out of his hands, turning red. "I—"

But I cut him off. He didn't have to explain. "I told you I could wander between universes. That's how the mirror works. I guess I just disappear. I've never been here when I went through, so I don't really know what it looks like from this side. I just go into it. I mean, I guess."

"Did you get through? Does time stay the same when you go into the mirror? Like did an entire day pass for you but for me it was only a few seconds? That would be so cool. You could live forever that way."

I smiled at the excitement in Jamie's eyes but shook my head.

"I didn't get through. I think time stays the same when I go through the mirror. I'm pretty sure I can only get all the way through if Samara is actually looking in the mirror. The first time I went through, I had to break a mirror to get in. I think that was like breaking down the door on my side, and then I stepped out on Samara's side because my end of the world was shattered into pieces on the floor.

"There's something that stops me sometimes but not other times. I don't know for sure what it is, but I think I can't get through the mirror unless Samara is looking in a mirror somewhere. It makes sense that she would be avoiding the mirror now if she's mad at me." I paused and thought about it. "Or scared of me."

The idea that she might be scared of me upset me, but I caught myself when I remembered that Jamie was there. "So instead, I got stuck between our worlds in this black box that has nothing. I mean no light, but also no emotion, no anything. And until Samara looks in the mirror at me, that's as far as I can get."

It was a long-winded explanation and I wasn't sure that it was right, but it made sense to me at the time and Jamie accepted it as being logical. At least as logical as anything in this weird double world.

I started pacing the room, looking for something that would give me a clue and fiddling with a pen I had picked up off my desk. I turned around and saw Jamie lying on the floor tossing a ball up and down. I stuck the pen in my hair and watched for a minute as the ball went up and hit the edge of the dream catcher that hung over my bed.

"What's that?"

"A dream catcher. I don't know why it's still up there. I made it a really long time ago." It was one of those wooden and string things that I had made when I was in elementary school, and it had been above my bed ever since.

Jamie sat up and didn't seem to notice the ball bounce off the top of his head and roll away. "Dreams!"

"Dreams?" I asked.

"Maybe you can get to her dreams through the black box. And then you can talk to her. She can't control what she dreams, so she'll have to listen to you."

"How do I get there, though?" I asked, sitting down and leaning on the edge of my bed. Jamie walked over to the edge of my bed to get the ball and leaned against the bed, starting to toss the ball up again. "I mean, what if I get stuck in the black box and I can never get out again and I have to live in the empty space?"

The ball went up. "Could you use the black box like a touch tunnel?" The ball hit his hand and went up in the air again. "Like at a kids' museum or a science museum or something." Down. Up. "Keep one hand on the wall next to you…" Down, up. "And if you get lost, just turn around and walk back." Jamie held the ball for a second. Then up again. "If it doesn't work, you'll come back…" Down, up. "And we'll come up with a new plan."

I leaned over and grabbed the ball before Jamie could catch it. I fell over onto him, and he put his arms around me for a second. Then we both looked at each other and moved away again. I sat up.

"It's a good idea," I said, "but, well…I can't wander into her dreams. I mean, how would you feel if someone saw your dreams?" Jamie nodded and lay back down holding the ball still for a moment. I sat down next to him. "Jamie, I just want to say thanks. For, you know, believing me and being here."

I could tell he wanted to say something so I propped my chin up on his knees. "What?"

"Nothing, I just worry about you."

"I'll be fine," I said, touching his arm. "This isn't dangerous, just difficult." He sat up for a second and I knew he wanted to say something, so it was the perfect time for my mom to walk in. She looked at me, then at Jamie, who immediately turned beet red, then back at me. I sat up straight and turned to face her.

"Hi, sweetheart, I'm home." There was a really awkward pause. It's like when you're watching a really clean movie and the moment that it gets the tiniest bit raunchy is always the moment that someone's parents walk in. The movie can be an animated fairy tale, but someone's parents always walk in just as the prince is kissing the princess and breaking the spell. "Is your friend—"

"Jamie, Mom."

"Jamie…" She corrected herself, regained her composure, and smiled at him. "Staying for dinner?" He shook his head and stood up.

"I've got to get going." He winked. "I'll see you at school tomorrow, though."

ॐ

After dinner that night, I sat and stared into the mirror in my bathroom for a long time. My reflection looked strangely different from Samara. I recognized her as being my reflection, but for some reason she looked very different to me. I started to wonder who I saw when Samara wasn't on the other side and who my mom saw since Samara's mom was dead.

I flashed back to something my mother had told me years earlier. She'd said that the face in the mirror is very different from the face everyone else sees when they look at you. That how you see yourself is nothing like what others see when they look at you. I tried to figure out whether my reflection was what everyone else saw or what only I saw.

Was Samara what I wanted to see? Or what everyone else wanted to see? I leaned back on the door frame of the closet and closed my eyes for a minute. I wanted to know the answers to these questions for myself as much as for Samara, but I wasn't sure that there was a way to find out.

I pressed my head against the cool glass of the mirror for a moment and leaned backward, standing up to walk toward my bed. I took one last look, and there she was, all of a sudden, standing in front of me. I took advantage of the moment, immediately stepping through the mirror.

I came out in her bathroom and immediately turned the corner into her room. I didn't notice until I walked up behind her, but I was crying. I had been up most of the night as I waited for her, but just seeing her the way she was, so scared and upset, left me upset too.

"I'm so sorry, Samara. I won't lie to you again. I didn't mean to do this. It just happened and then I didn't want to tell you because I thought you wouldn't understand, so I didn't tell you and then…I never meant to hurt you. I wanted…I wanted you to be the sister I always wished I had. Please, please trust me."

Samara fell into my arms, and I felt our hearts pounding in sync. I promised not to leave her, not to go anywhere, to tell her the truth about everything I knew. I told her everything I could about the mirror, about going back and forth between worlds. But there was still a lot I didn't understand about it. We both had a lot of unanswered questions.

We talked all the time after that. About the most amazing and the most miniscule things.

"How is it going with Jamie?" Samara asked during one of our talks one day.

I wasn't sure how it was going with Jamie. I still wasn't one hundred percent sure how I felt about him, though the more time we spent together, the more I liked him.

"I guess it's good. I don't know. Why?"

"You talk about him a lot. It seems like maybe there's something…happening with you two. Is there?"

"I don't know," I said. I paused for a second. "I hope so," I added, and I heard myself giggle. Hearing myself giggle that way, I knew I liked him more than I had been telling myself I did.

"Oh, come on, everything you say about him. He obviously likes you. Get a move on! Get it together with him." She pursed her lips and smiled, turning her head a little to the side. It was the knowing smile she gave me whenever I talked about Jamie.

"Don't push," I told her. "If it's going to happen, it's going to happen. I don't want to pressure him or anything." In the back of my mind, I did want to start pushing things. I didn't want to lose a friend I had had for such a long time. But I didn't want to lose a chance with a guy I really cared about either.

I hardly had any experience with boys. I was good with girls. I could get along with almost any of them. But I had no idea how to talk to guys. I started to wonder about getting Samara into my world, into a place where she could meet him and help me figure out what to do. By switching places with Samara, I could help patch things up with her dad, and maybe she could help me figure out the next steps with Jamie.

I put off asking her about it for a little while. I needed to know that she would be able to handle it. Switching lives seemed like a crazy idea to me, and I had already spent time in both worlds. So we continued meeting every night to talk for hours on end.

One night, while Samara sat sipping her milk and I nibbled

on cookies, she asked me, "Do you think the alternate universes are something we should share? Maybe we aren't meant to be the only ones who know about them."

That was the first time I wondered if other people were sitting up until all hours of the morning talking to their reflections. If enough people were, I wondered if we would be able to just start talking to each other without hiding it anymore.

"I'm afraid the people in our worlds might clash if they met," I admitted to Samara.

Samara agreed tentatively, and the two of us wondered together if they'd want to use each other for medical experiments or something. "All the people would get all mixed up," Samara said, "and you would never know who you were talking to. What if they went to war?"

"That would be so crazy," she said, "if all these people who kind of look like each other but not quite started, like, fist-fighting and stuff."

"And then the only way you could tell someone from their reflection would be by whose nose was broken?"

"Or whose arm was in a sling?"

"And the worlds got all messed up and crazy?" I asked, laughing. She started to laugh too, and we were both consumed by fits of laughter that were so intense we couldn't talk for a few minutes.

When we got our composure back, we agreed that we wouldn't tell anyone else, and I was glad Jamie already knew. I wanted to be able to talk about it with him, but if he hadn't already known, I couldn't have broken my promise to Samara.

I asked Samara later that night what had happened to her mom. I could tell when she told me that she was blaming herself. I wished she didn't. But her eyes told me so, and it was an intense and overwhelming experience to see the pain in her eyes. Her mother was still so much alive in her.

She brought out the shirt she had been wearing the day she found her mom. It was stained, she said, in the exact places there was blood on her mom's shirt. I believed her. I believed that it was a sign from her mom, but I didn't know what it meant. I didn't know why it was the way it was. And I didn't know what to say to her when she told me.

All I could do was try to comfort her. It didn't feel like nearly enough. She was hurting so badly, and I wanted to do something, something that would help her. I could see the death happening over and over and over in Samara's mind.

Finally I decided to ask. I had been thinking about switching places for days, and I needed to know what Samara would think about it.

"Samara, let's switch places." We were sitting in our respective bedrooms. It was funny that Samara looked brighter than me for the first time. My mom had asked me to keep the lights off when I didn't need them because of the winter electricity bills, and Samara had the light in her closet on. The right half of her face was lit up by the closet light, and her left half was silhouetted against a long red dress.

She dismissed the idea of switching immediately, but as I

pushed her to think about it more seriously, I could see her getting excited. A lot of me wanted to see what Samara's life was really like. I was curious who she talked to when I wasn't there and what she did with her time. But at least a small, very selfish part of me wanted to see what she could figure out about Jamie and what he thought of me. Where things were going with him.

"I'm afraid of walking into the mirror. I'm afraid that I'm going to screw up your life."

"I'll help you come through," I promised, "and as far as screwing up my life, there are three people I care about. You, my mother—"

"And Jamie," she finished for me.

"Right, and you'll know, Jamie will know, and my mother is my mother. There is nothing you could do to make her not like me. She loves me unconditionally."

"From what you've told me, Jamie does too." There was that smile again, but it faded after a moment. "I wish I had two people in my life like that."

"Samara, I'm sure you do. You just don't see it. I'm sure it's there. You have at least one," I said, smiling at her. "So does that mean you'll do it? We'll switch lives?"

She gave it a moment of thought. "Yes, let's do it."

"Okay, meet me here tomorrow morning and we'll switch. I mean, we already know everything there is to know about each other, but in case there's a problem, we'll just check in all day. We'll just meet every hour on the hour. Okay?"

Samara nodded and blew me a kiss good night.

❧

The next morning I got ready for the switch between worlds, feeling sure that I had forgotten something. I tried to dress how I imagined Samara might be dressed so people wouldn't be able to tell it was me. I wondered as I pulled a dark green shirt over my head what it would be like to pretend to be Samara. And how Samara would do at pretending to be me. I believed what I had told her the night before, though, that there wasn't really anything she could screw up so badly that I couldn't undo it. The people I cared about would be with me regardless of any mistakes Samara made.

I met Samara at the bedroom mirrors. She was already there when I got there. She asked me to hold her hand while she walked through, but I wasn't sure if she would have the same amazing experience I had the first time if I was anchoring her, so I insisted she walk through herself.

"You don't need my help. Just breathe and step in, and you'll be okay." I watched as she took a deep breath and closed her eyes tightly. She took a step forward and was replaced for a moment by my soulless reflection.

I stepped in as well and tried to call to her as I walked through: "Open your eyes. It's beautiful. You don't want to miss this."

I didn't know if she could hear me or not, but I figured it was worth a shot. I felt my whole body start tingling in a way it had never done before. I stepped out of the mirror into Samara's bedroom and turned to see her standing on my faded blue carpet.

Samara already looked happier. Her cheeks were flushed and bright. There was a sparkle in her green eyes…she didn't look like Samara. She looked like…me. We had taken each other's bodies.

Samara looked down at her hands and then back up at me. "Oh, my God," she whispered. "We did it. I'm really here. We're really here. Anything I should know—any last-minute tips?" I tried to think of anything she needed to know, but I could already hear my mom calling her in the background.

"Lorna? Where are you?"

"Who's Lorna?" Samara asked me.

"I am. I mean, you are. That's my real name. When I was little, my dad used to call me Lorna Doone, like the cookie. It caught at school, and at some point I just became Doone, then Dee. But Mom still uses Lorna. She doesn't like using a name that my dad gave me. Now go. She's calling you. We'll check in about an hour from now. Good luck, Samara—I mean Dee!"

We left the mirror at the same time, but I could feel concern mounting in the back of my mind that I'd forgotten something. I had left everything for school. I'd cleaned my room. I'd left notes about what was in my bag. We had talked about where to sit in classes and what to say to my mom. But something was bothering me...

I looked at Samara's room in the light for the first time and took a deep breath. Whatever I had forgotten, there was nothing I could do about it now. The only time I had been in Samara's room was the night I'd spent convincing her to talk to me. I had been too preoccupied then to see anything. Now I had nothing else to do. I was alone in her room; I had the time to explore and to find out as much about Samara as I could. It was like looking at Samara's life in a bottle. I took in the colors, the textures, the things.

She had a soft beige carpet and light blue walls with a dark blue border on the top and bottom. Her gray desk took up most of a wall and was cluttered with papers, notebooks, open pens, and stretched-out hair ties. I found a picture of her and her mother on the table next to her bed. Her mom looked just like Samara. And really similar to what my mom had looked like when I was younger. Samara must have been six or seven, and her mom was smiling. In a way her mom looked happy, but she had bags under her eyes and was obviously worn out.

Samara had another cabinet that matched her gray desk. I opened the door. The cabinet was split in half by a vertical board. On one side was an assortment of lipsticks, blushes, nail polishes, hair bands, and cotton balls. On the other side was a clutter of things. I sat cross-legged in front of the cabinet and began taking everything out.

The first layer of stuff included a mirror, seven handles to razors—which seemed like bizarre keepsakes, a flower, and a ticket to a school dance. Behind that, there were a few empty dime bags, a bowl, and a picture of her kissing a guy I didn't recognize and holding a bottle of coconut rum. I guess I wasn't surprised. I knew Samara had a wild side. I was just glad she was moving away from that now. I thought I was fine with it, but I couldn't imagine seeing Samara acting like that.

There was a history test she had gotten an A- on dated the same day as the picture. When I took those out, I found a sketchbook full of drawings of floor-length dresses, a picture of Samara when she was about eleven sitting on a tire swing in her backyard, and a small boy's baseball cap. Behind those was a nearly complete set of *The Baby-Sitter's Club* books and two small, gorgeous porcelain dolls.

The last thing in the cabinet was a sign that must have been written by Samara when she was really young that said, "No matter how mad you get, never disappoint Mommy and Daddy and don't ever make them cry." I looked at the sign for a moment and wondered when was the last time Samara had seen it.

I turned from the sign and saw a clock on Samara's bedside table. I had to get to school. I stood up and walked out of Samara's room.

"Dad?"

There was no answer. I hadn't expected one, but I had hoped that there would be. I took a deep breath, rolled up my sleeves, and prepared to leave the house. This wouldn't be my first time at Samara's school, but it would be my first time trying to *be* Samara. What if I wasn't able to do it? Or what if I was and it just showed me that Samara's life was really terrible? Or that it was wonderful?

I pulled out a little hand mirror and looked at my reflection. Samara wasn't there, but I noticed that her hair was straightened and in a ponytail. I went into the bathroom, pulled the ponytail out, and threw my head under the sink. I flipped it back, and as I wrapped a towel around my hair, trying to dry it as quickly as possible, I noticed a scar on Samara's arm.

Without thinking, I ran the fingers of my other hand over it and then up my arm, and I found another one.

And another.

My heartbeat pushed up a notch. I pulled my shirt off over my head. Samara's arms were covered with scars, new and old. Some of them were still welts that hadn't even scarred over yet. Those were from the last few days, maybe even the last twenty-four hours. Between new and old scars, it seemed like half the skin of her shoulder had been peeled off. I stared at the rough patches of skin and caressed the scars with my fingers. I looked at my hands touching the scars in the mirror and realized my cheeks were streaked with mascara-y tears.

chapter 5

Sinking In

Samara in Dee's World

When I was in science in eighth grade, I learned that there are colors that we can't see because of their wavelengths. They're brighter and of a completely different type than the colors we usually see. Like if you shined a black light or an ultraviolet light on everything for a second. But those colors were in addition to the colors I see every day. I saw them, all of those colors, when I walked through the mirror.

By the time I stepped out into Dee's world, she was already on my side of the mirror. We stared at each other for a moment, I think both realizing that we had taken each other's bodies and wondering if we had just done something really, really dumb.

We tried to give each other last-minute tips, but Dee's tips scared me more than comforted me because, as it turned out, I hadn't even known Dee's real name before we switched. I immediately began wondering what else I didn't know about her. And what else she didn't know about me. But I could hear Dee's mom calling me, and I knew I didn't have time to really worry about it right then. I had to go be Dee. Or Lorna.

"Turn off your light on the way out of the room," she called to me. I walked into the kitchen and stopped dead in my tracks.

"Ms. Herwitz?" I blurted out before regaining my composure.

She looked at me strangely for a moment, and I was afraid she would remember where the name was from or when people had called her that. But I recovered.

"Sorry…I had a weird dream last night. Anyway. Good morning—" I felt the name choke in my throat. I hadn't said it in so long that it hurt coming out. "Good morning, Mom." She perked up and smiled, placing a bowl of cereal in front of me before cutting up a banana into some yogurt for herself.

"Anything special going on at school today?" she asked me.

"Umm…" I didn't want to lie to her. "Not that I know of?"

"Sweetheart, don't bring your voice up at the end of your sentences. It gives you less conviction when you talk."

Conviction was the last thing I had right then but I nodded, not wanting to risk accidentally asking another question when I responded to her. We sat in silence for a few minutes while Dee's mom read the paper and I poked at my cereal. I wasn't very hungry. I tried to think of something to say, something that would start a conversation with her, just to hear her voice. This was Dee's mom, but it was my mom's reflection too. This was the woman my mom saw when she looked in the mirror. But all I could come up with was, "Anything special going on at work today?"

She laughed. Her smile was so beautiful. "One of the things about being a nurse is that you really don't know if there's anything special going on until it starts."

I smiled, thinking it must be an exciting job. I had forgotten she was a nurse. I still thought of her as an English teacher. I looked at the faded tablecloth and wondered what it was like to work for a doctor you could never afford to go to.

"You don't seem like yourself," she said, looking over the paper at me for a moment. "Is anything wrong?"

"No," I said, and I meant it. I was sitting at breakfast with Mom, having—or trying to have—a full meal before I left for school. Dee's mom knew her well enough to realize that I wasn't acting like Dee's self. I sat thinking about Dee's mom and about my mom. I wondered if they were similar or if they were exact opposites, like me and Dee. There were so many questions I wanted to ask my own mother, but I couldn't. This could be the closest I would get...

"Tell me again, Mom, what were you like as a teenager? You grew up here, didn't you? Was the neighborhood still the same?"

"Lorna, you've heard these stories a hundred times," she said, looking up at me. "Why are you asking again now?"

"I just like picturing you as a kid...like me."

She looked, folded her arms, furrowed her eyebrow, and licked her lips. "Well," she said, "I was a lot like you in high school. I loved high school, just like you do." *I hate high school.* "I contributed to the lit magazine, but I wasn't assistant editor, like you." *I get out of school as quickly as possible, no after-school activities.* "I was really close to my mom," she said with a smile, but all I could think was *I don't have a mom.* "I used to love horses when I was little. I wanted to learn to ride, to compete." I saw the past in her eyes. I saw her watching horses gallop around a park nearby.

"But you know how things are. Never happened. Maybe as a retirement present to myself." She smiled at me. "Finish up. Come on, you've got to get going soon."

I took a deep breath. There was one question I hadn't been able to ask Dee, and more than anything I wanted to know the answer. "Mom?"

"Hmm?" she said absentmindedly.

"Someone did a story about her parents for the lit mag, and it made me wonder…I mean, I couldn't remember…how did you and Dad meet?"

She put the paper down next to her and sighed, brushing her hand along her cheek. She turned away, and I couldn't tell if I saw a tear in her eye. I'm sure I imagined it because when she turned back, it wasn't there.

"Not now, Lorna. I don't know why you're asking all of these questions all of a sudden. I'll tell you that story again another time, okay? Just get ready for school. You're going to be late."

"Yeah," I said, stumbling over my words, "I'm sorry. I didn't mean to…"

"That's okay. This just isn't the time."

I got up quickly. I hadn't meant to upset her. I cleared the table and grabbed Dee's bag from her room. She had left it right next to the bed for me, fully packed for the day. On my way out the door, Dee's mom stopped me to give me a kiss.

"Have a good day, sweetheart."

"Thanks," I felt it stick in my throat again, "Mom."

❧

Dee's neighborhood was just as easy to navigate as she'd said it would be. It was a lot like my neighborhood, the epicenter of a couple of different suburbs. The local high school was within walking distance from her house, and like mine, it was fed by middle schools in a couple of other neighborhoods.

When I walked out the door, I ran directly into a steady stream of students. I walked with them down the street, trying to make landmarks for myself so I could find my way home at the end of the day. I followed the crowd toward the school, accidentally taking a detour with older kids who were dropping off siblings at elementary and middle schools.

When I was about to walk through the building, I heard someone call, "Dee!" I took a deep breath and smiled as I turned to watch a girl in a deep pink velour tracksuit run toward me.

"Hey, sweetie," I said, leaning in for an air kiss and doing my best to look as carefree as Dee would have been at seeing this girl.

The girl seemed to catch the eye of someone behind me and hurried up a little. "Sorry to bug you. I just wanted to check if you finished looking over the pieces for 'The Brick Bard.' I want to start getting it laid out this afternoon."

I stared into my bag emptily for a moment, silently wondering if I would be able to recognize what she was talking about.

"Umm, I'm not sure if I remembered…" I trailed off because there was a Post-it sticking up from a CD with "LitMag—for Kelly" written on it.

"Sure, here you go," I said, pulling it out and desperately

hoping she was Kelly. I felt the tension build in my back for a second. But when she smiled and took it, I felt myself relax again.

"Thanks a million," she said, and bounced away toward a group of girls who looked exactly like her, plus or minus the color of the velour.

I couldn't believe I had pulled it off. I'd had practice pretending to be a happy-go-lucky girl, but never like this. But that girl had no idea that I wasn't Dee; as far as she was concerned, I was the one who'd edited those stories or poems or whatever was on that CD I'd given her.

I looked up at the clock behind the entrance and realized that it was time for my first check-in with the real Dee. I slipped into a bathroom stall and pulled out a hand mirror. Hopefully anyone who overheard would just think I was talking on my phone. When I looked in the mirror, Dee was already there.

"What are these about, Samara?" she asked, pulling back my sleeves. She had found the cuts. I had been so wrapped up in thinking about myself being Dee, looking like her, acting like her, that I'd forgotten that she had become me too.

"What are these? How long have you been doing this? Ever since we've been friends? Since before that? I can't believe you kept this from me."

"It's…" I sputtered, and Dee finally made eye contact with me. What was I going to say it was—a hobby? "It's an addiction. I couldn't help it. It started a long time ago. And once I started…"

Dee sounded angry, but her eyes looked like she had been crying. "You know what, Samara? I can't deal with this right now.

We have to keep pretending to be each other. We can talk about this when we both get home tonight, okay? But, well, no, never mind. Tonight."

I nodded, too stunned and ashamed to say anything. I noticed that Dee had changed how I wore my hair. She always wore hers in curls, and today mine was down and curly too. It fell better on her than it ever had on me. She had forgotten to put on my makeup too. Before I could ask her about it, she had put away the pocket mirror and my real reflection, two-dimensional and with empty eyes, was back.

"Shit."

❧

I got full force into Dee's life as soon as I started going to her classes. School was almost fun when so many people wanted to sit with me and talk to me. I followed Dee's instructions and sat in the third row, second seat from the left in every class.

A girl I didn't know sat down next to me in the first class. "Hey," she said.

I smiled. "Hi. How ya doin'?" I asked, finding it easier to ask the questions than to answer them.

"Good. Lot of work last night so I'm, ugh…" she leaned her head back, "…exhausted. I don't know how you do lit mag too."

"It's not so bad," I said, really meaning it. Being Dee wasn't bad at all.

I raised my hand in two of my morning classes, which I would never have done in my own school. And another two times, I got called on out of nowhere. I didn't flinch. I answered.

I checked in with Dee again before lunch. "I just realized what I forgot," she said, and I could hear the urgency in her voice.

"What? What is it?" I asked. But she was cut off. I guess someone else was coming because she disappeared and was replaced by the girl with empty eyes looking back at me. I sighed and went into the lunchroom. I was really curious what Dee had forgotten, but I was feeling great and figured I would be able to handle it, whatever it was. I *was* Dee.

I turned and was on my way into the cafeteria when Kelly, the girl in the pink tracksuit, called me over to tell me Jamie was looking for me. I began looking around for him, but then I felt a hand on my back and someone whispered, "Follow me." I followed Jamie out one of the back doors of the school. We walked without talking but I was so grateful to be with someone who knew who I was that I appreciated the break from thinking about who I wasn't.

He was attractive, but in a quiet way. Some people are attractive in that way where you can't tear your eyes off them as they walk down the street, and some people, like Jamie, are just nice to look at. He had olive-colored skin and freckles. Most of his freckles were on the right side of his face, so he looked like his head was constantly cocked a little to the side even though it wasn't.

He brought me to a park a few blocks from the school, and I wondered if we were allowed to leave school during lunch. I doubted that Dee's school had open lunch, but I didn't think Jamie would purposely use the fact that it was me instead of Dee to get her into trouble. I noticed that it was starting to get chilly.

The seasons were just changing so the weather had that crisp feel without actually feeling cold yet.

We sat down on the ground in the park and I looked at Jamie, wondering what he had brought me here for, if there was something Dee had wanted him to tell me outside of school. I looked into his eyes, and for a moment I couldn't put my finger on what was wrong.

"Jamie, are you stoned? Isn't it a little early?"

"A little. But everything is really clear," he said, closing his eyes and shaking his head backward. His hair fell just so, dropping back to exactly the same place every time he shook his head, so it seemed a little bit silly to keep doing it. He sat down next to me on the ground, saying, "Look, Dee, I know—"

"Wait a minute—" I tried to cut him off.

"No, just let me say this first."

"But—"

"No, don't. Just please let me." He put his hands on my cheeks and leaned toward me. And he kissed me. I had never been kissed like that before. Not with that kind of love or even with that kind of passion. He really cared about me; he loved me. I felt myself sinking into him, sinking into the kiss, and I had to remind myself that the feeling was not for me. He didn't love *me*. People don't love *me*. I pulled back from him.

"Dee, I'm...I'm sorry. I didn't..."

"No, it's...Jamie, I'm not Dee." I looked around and lowered my voice. "I'm Samara. Dee said she told you we were switching for the day."

"Oh, shit. Shit. Fuck." He pulled his knees up to his chest and ran his fingers through his hair. He squeezed his eyes shut tightly and rubbed one hand over his face, while he tapped his knee with his other thumb.

I put my hand on his knee. "I'm sorry. You didn't let me tell you. And, I mean, I thought you knew. Dee told me…she told me that she'd told you."

"It's okay," he said, looking up at me blearily. "You didn't…just don't…let me tell her, okay? I want to be able to tell her myself. I've been waiting all this time to tell her, trying to come up with the perfect place and way, and…and, oh shit."

He banged one hand against the ground and fell backward onto the grass. I heard a few leaves crunch underneath him. I could see him cooling off, though the bright white color of his knuckles was still distinct against the grass underneath them. He took a few deep breaths, then sat up and did his best to smile at me.

"Well, welcome to my world," he said with a hint of sarcasm in his voice. "How's your day been so far?"

"I took one step forward and found out what it's like to have a mom who waits for me to finish breakfast before leaving for the day and cares whether I go to school or not, friends who actually like spending time with me, and a boy who's in love with me. My life is feeling pretty bleak right now. But I guess Dee's day is looking up."

I tried to smile and Jamie tried to smile back. We sat there for a minute. I don't think either of us quite knew what to do with the other. Finally Jamie broke the silence.

"Come on, let's go have lunch. My treat. Least I can do for, well, for mixing the two of you up."

"Oh, you don't have to do that. Thanks, though."

"Well then, let's go have lunch just because..."

"Because you have the munchies?"

Jamie smiled and got up, grabbing my hand and pulling me up with him.

We went to a pizza place nearby and ran into a bunch of Jamie's friends. I sat with them for lunch, but while we were walking back toward school, Kelly came over and asked to "steal me" for a second.

"So," she said, "come on. Spill. I saw you walking off with Jamie. What happened?"

I wasn't sure what to tell her, but her arm was linked so tightly with mine that I didn't think I had the option of not responding. Eventually my hand would have fallen off due to lack of circulation.

"Nothing, he just wanted to ask me something about the homework we were doing together." I tried to fake disappointment without being too obvious about it. I wasn't sure what Kelly knew about Dee and Jamie, and I didn't want to be the one to start rumors.

I couldn't help thinking about that kiss, and it left my head in such a fog that I barely noticed the rest of the day passing. Fortunately the people around me seemed content with smiling and nodding at appropriate times and didn't mind that I wasn't talking much. I had never been kissed the way Jamie kissed me—kissed *Dee*, the way he had kissed Dee. The same voice in the back of my head that had driven me to look for Dee again was making me wonder if it would be possible to make that kind of kiss happen again.

What would I tell Dee about what happened? I hated to keep anything else from her, especially something that would make her so happy. And we had agreed not to keep secrets. But then I ran into Jamie and he asked me again not to tell her. The earnest look in his eyes sucked me in. I couldn't take that moment away from him. He wanted to tell her himself. I felt like I should respect that.

"No, I won't tell her."

"Thanks," he said. "I owe you one. Am I going to see you tomorrow?"

I shrugged. "Your guess is as good as mine. But if Dee is back tomorrow—I mean, if the two of us don't see each other again—then I need to say this now." I pulled on his arm to stop him from moving and turned him to face me. "Don't hurt her. Dee is a wonderful person. She's loving and trusting and sweet. You don't have the right to hurt her, okay?"

"Don't worry," he told me. "I couldn't imagine hurting Dee."

"Good."

❧

Unfortunately, Jamie was the first thing Dee asked me about that night. I think she just needed something to ease me into the conversation we were about to have. We were in each other's rooms. We owned the same pajamas, and I know it must sound weird, but it was funny having my reflection look like me while we were sitting there. She had lit a candle in my room that illuminated her. The side of her face that was closer to me anyway.

"I forgot to tell Jamie. I forgot to tell him you were coming. Was everything okay? Did you explain it to him?"

"I told him. Don't worry about it."

"Did he say anything about me? Do you think he might like me?"

I paused. I didn't want to lie, but I had promised Jamie that I wouldn't say anything. "He, well, yeah, I think he might like you. He'll probably make a move soon. I mean, I think."

She smiled and sat up a little straighter.

"Did he say anything?"

"He just said he...wants to talk to you when you get back," I said, shrugging and trying to look nonchalant. If he wanted to tell her, I wanted to let him. And maybe...maybe he wouldn't. I tried to drive that thought out of my head.

We sat silently for what felt like an eternity after Dee asked about Jamie. We avoided making eye contact. I played with the fringe of the rug in her room.

Finally Dee took a deep breath and said, "I understand, Samara. For the first time, I understand that this..." she ran my hand along my thigh, "...is an addiction. But that makes it all the more important that you get help stopping."

"I don't need help. Dee, I haven't thought about cutting all day. Not even once. I'm kicking it already. I don't need help."

"I don't believe you. And I don't think I can help you. I think this is too big for me to help you with alone. I have to tell your dad, Sam. I'm sorry."

What right did she have to tell anyone anything? "You don't have to. You don't have to *do* anything. All you have to do is let me handle this, let me deal with it myself."

"You'll never stop if I let you deal with it yourself," Dee said. "It's too addicting. You're not going to be able to stop doing this without help. I'm going to help you."

I had kicked habits before. Dee had never even tried. She had never needed that kind of release, that kind of outlet. What did she know about it? I couldn't imagine what made her think she was the expert in this.

"It's like I told you. I haven't thought about cutting all day. There's no reason to get my father involved in this whole thing. He can barely handle himself, let alone other people. Believe me, if you put my dad in charge of my addiction, it's going to take ages longer than if I just deal with it myself."

"I know you can't see it now, but I'm trying to help. My mind is made up. You'll be glad I did this when you're better."

"That's bullshit and you know it," I said quietly, staring into the flickering flame of the candle sitting next to Dee. "When's the last time you heard someone actually thank someone else later?"

Dee's shoulders slumped. "I'm sorry, Samara. But I won't let you hurt yourself anymore." She blew out the candle and walked away.

I sat in front of the mirror for a few minutes longer and gaped at Dee's reflection, not knowing what to do.

chapter 6

Couldn't Tell the Difference

Dee in Samara's World

I couldn't believe that through all of the time that Samara and I had been struggling, she had never told me that she was dealing with this huge thing. It had been close to a month of talking every single night. She had been cutting herself the entire time (based on the number of scars). She had never told me she was *this* unhappy. I'd thought I knew what was going on with her. I'd thought she was being honest with me, and obviously she wasn't.

I decided to leave for school, even though I wanted to stay home and sit in the dark replaying every conversation Samara and I had ever had. I wanted to look for clues that this had been going on. But I knew that, given everything else, Samara did *not* need to skip more classes and have that on her record.

I'd thought it was going to be easy. I had been to Samara's school before, and I had seen everyone there. But I was so involved in how Samara and I would get along when I was there the first time that I hadn't really been focused on her friendships with other people. I'd assumed when we talked that she was exaggerating how lonely she was. After all, the two of us picked up so easily that it was hard to imagine other people having trouble getting along with her. I hadn't seen her sitting with anyone, but I also hadn't been looking. It was easier for me to approach her when she was alone anyway.

As I walked to school, my mind raced over the cuts I had found on Samara's arms, hips, and legs. If she had kept that from me, I could hardly imagine her talking to the prissy girls at school about her life. That's why I was particularly happy to turn around to a familiar face when someone called, "Samara." The girl was pretty and had short brown hair and big eyes. She motioned to her friends to wait for her for a minute and came over.

"I just wanted to say," she glanced back at her friends, "you look good today. I mean, I like your hair like that. Down and I don't know...natural like that. It's like you used to wear it when we were little."

"Eva, come on," someone called to her.

She smiled for a moment before turning back to her friends and calling, "God, chill. I'm coming already."

Samara's classes were easy to get through. She had told me to take the back right corner of each class, and I did. Her teachers never called on me, and given all that was on my mind, I didn't particularly want to raise my hand and have to fake Samara. In class, I often found myself absentmindedly running my hands over the scars that were hidden underneath my clothes.

I dreaded going to lunch. The only person I knew was Eva, and she didn't seem like someone Samara would sit and talk to for an hour. It didn't sound like they got along. I wondered what had happened between the two of them that made it that way, since Eva seemed perfectly nice to me.

Maybe I could fix things with Eva. Then Samara would have someone to talk to in this world too. Someone to walk to school with and to sit with at lunch. And then, in a while, if Samara wanted to, it would be okay if she told Eva about the mirror. That way she would have someone like Jamie to talk to.

Jamie! That's when I realized: I'd forgotten to tell Jamie that Samara and I were switching places for the day. I trusted Samara to tell him, but she was supposed to not have to deal with this. She was supposed to be finding out what was going on with him for me.

As soon as Samara got to the mirror for our first check-in of the day, I said, "I just realized what I forgot."

"What?"

But before I could explain, a group of guys walked by and I had to shut the mirror. As difficult as school was for her, she didn't need people thinking she talked to herself. That certainly wouldn't be helpful. One of them gave me a very knowing look. Something about the way he looked at me made me really uncomfortable, and I wondered how well he and Samara knew each other.

I sat alone at lunch, nibbling lightly at the salad I had gotten. I was alone in my classes for the rest of the day. I had hoped that I would get home and find Samara's dad there, at least for some company, someone to talk to who I wouldn't feel so self-conscious around.

Samara hadn't made it to any of our hourly check-ins for the rest of the day. I wasn't worried; I figured she would be okay in my world. There was very little that she could do to really screw things up. But it would've been nice to have a little support being her. I was shocked to find that it was as bad as she'd said it was.

When I got back to Samara's house, there was a note on the kitchen table that said, "Money for dinner under the plates. Back late. Love, Dad." Great, I thought. Besides being lonely all day, now I have to sit in this giant echoey house all night. I felt completely empty.

I went up to the bathroom and, without thinking, picked up a razor and put a slit in the top of my arm. Then another. The first thing to register was the smell of blood. Then the deep red color on my arm. And a moment later, the pain. I stared at my hand, my terrible hand that had just done this. It looked foreign to me. I couldn't believe that was my hand, *Samara's hand,* that had just put a cut into my arm, *Samara's arm.* Mine. Samara's. I couldn't tell the difference between them anymore. I had done this without thinking, without knowing what I was doing. And now without regret because it felt so damn good.

The house seemed somehow smaller, less intimidating. School seemed farther away. I had had a stomachache all day that I hadn't noticed, but I was very aware that it was gone now. I stared at my hand and sank down to the floor. What had I done?

∽

I had to decide what to do before I saw Samara that night. Would I tell her that I had cut myself? Was it that she had cut herself? I felt like a bystander. I didn't feel like *I* had done it. I had never been addicted to something before; I had never known what it was like to do something compulsively or to not be able to stop myself.

I heard the phone ring and wanted to peel myself off the floor but I just couldn't. I listened to the third ring and accepted that I wasn't going to get it. After the fifth ring I heard the answering machine beep. The door was open, so it was easy to hear from the second floor. I heard little Samara say, "We're not home, but you can leave a message after the tone." I heard the beep.

"Sam? You home yet? Okay, well, like I said, I'll be working late today. I have to meet the West Coast VP after work but I'll be home as soon as I can. There's money for dinner. Okay, see you later."

I stared down at the blood on the floor. If it hadn't been me, hadn't been my hand, my arm, I wouldn't have believed that cutting was even something that a person could be addicted to. But it *was* me. I watched the blood flowing down; I felt the intense relief at the same time that I felt intense shame. It was me; I had done all of it. And I knew it was wrong.

I knew better than to mutilate my own body and, even worse, to mutilate somebody else's body. This body was on loan. Samara's arms weren't mine to cut. Not that she should cut her own arms either, but I wasn't going to be the one with the scars I had just made. And I had made them anyway.

I wanted so badly to show Samara that her life was fine. That the problems were in her head. But they weren't. It was as bad as she thought and maybe worse. As I stared at the cuts I had put into my arm, I knew that hadn't really made any of the problems go away. It had made me feel better but it hadn't fixed anything. Samara needed to look at what was actually wrong, and I wanted to help her do that. I wanted to stop her from hurting so badly.

I couldn't be with her all the time, and even if I could, I didn't really have control over Samara or her actions. Apparently I didn't even have control over my own actions. I had done this without realizing it. I couldn't handle this. I needed an adult involved.

When I'd thought all Samara needed was a friend, I could do that. I wanted to. But I didn't even know what the first step was toward making this better. I didn't know what she needed. I knew that I needed to talk to her dad. He had called to check in. He cared more than Samara thought he did. However hard it was for the two of them to talk, I knew he would listen, would want to help. He was still her father.

That night, I let Samara start the conversation by talking about Jamie. She knew—and I knew—that we had something more important to talk about. Something else, something huge. But to just sit down and start there was too hard. I had hoped that something would have happened, that she could tell me for sure that he liked me or, I guess, that he didn't. Just so I would know. But all she told me was, "I think he likes you. He wants to talk to you when you get back."

Samara didn't know that the cut I was staring at on her arm was mine, not hers. And as I ran my index finger over the cut I had made, I wanted to say so many things. I wanted to say I wasn't strong enough. I wanted to say I could only do so much.

I wanted to say I loved her, that I felt her pain, her suffering. But all I said was, "I understand."

She looked at me and I knew she didn't believe it. "For the first time, I understand this is an addiction. But that makes it all the more important that you get help stopping."

"I don't need help stopping. Dee, I haven't thought about cutting all day. Not even once."

But she could only say the things she said because she didn't know. She didn't know that I had done this. I had made this cut in her arm. It was me, and I knew that if I couldn't stop myself, as much as I wanted to, she wouldn't be able to do it alone.

I couldn't let her keep doing this. She had two arms and half a leg full of scabs and scars. "I'm sorry, Samara. But I won't let you keep hurting yourself." I couldn't look at her anymore; it hurt too much to see her anger and her sadness and her pain. I blew out the candle that was lighting up the room and left the mirror. I hugged a pillow in Samara's bed and cried for close to an hour. I would have kept crying, but I ran out of tears.

I waited up for Samara's father that night. I knew if I didn't do it then, I never would. I sat on the couch in the living room in the dark for hours. Waiting. The cable box only flashed 12:00, so I don't know exactly how long it was. The room was big and my heart was beating so hard that I could hear it echo, especially when someone got close to the front steps of her townhouse.

I knew every inch of that room by the time Samara's father got home. I sat curled in the corner of the green leather couch, which was faded and worn from years of use. The couch was in the center of the room. In one corner behind it, an upright piano stood next to a huge window that took up most of the wall. The piano was covered in a layer of sad dust, showing that it hadn't been played in years. In front of me in one corner were a television and the cable box with the clock that wasn't set.

Next to the television was a fireplace with a mantel that held an assortment of pictures of Samara, her father, and her mother. The corner on the other side of the fireplace had a small stack of wood, showing that the fireplace had once been used. I could imagine a very distant past when a fire blazed and Samara and her father sat on the couch as her mother played piano, everyone smiling. But even those memories seemed to be covered by the same dust that covered the piano and the fireplace. They seemed unused, as if no one had even thought of them in years.

I shivered when I finally heard Samara's dad's car pull up. He turned on the light in the living room and jumped.

"Hi, Sam. What are you still doing up?"

"Hey," I said. "I couldn't sleep. There's some stuff we need to talk about. I need to tell you something. It's important."

"What is it?" he asked, crossing the room to sit next to me on the couch.

I knew that what I was about to say was going to devastate him. I knew I was bringing him news that he would be happier without. But I also knew that Samara could never be happy if her dad didn't know, if he couldn't help her get through this. And as bad as I felt for this balding older man my father had once seen in the mirror, I had to keep my promise to Samara to help her.

I pulled up my sleeve to show him Samara's arm. He immediately held onto my wrist and traced the scars. "What—?" But I interrupted his question.

"I've been cutting myself. I've been doing it for a long time, and I'm realizing now that I have to stop and I need you to help me."

He sighed heavily and pulled me close to hug me. He smelled like scotch. I was prepared for certain questions I thought he would ask: What's so wrong in your life, Samara? What made you think this was a good idea? But I don't think he understood enough to ask any of those questions.

"I'm going to help you through this," he said before his voice cracked. "I'm so sorry I didn't notice. I'm sorry I haven't taken better care of you, that I didn't take better care of your mother, and that she isn't here to help you."

I didn't want to hear about his guilt; that wasn't what was important. I wanted him to tell me what he would do for Samara to help her. "Don't be sorry. Look at me, Dad. I need you. Don't be sorry. Just don't let me down. Not again."

He looked shocked, and I felt shocked at the rage I had. It wasn't even my rage. I knew this was hard on him too, but all I could think was how angry I was that he was making this all about him.

"You're so strong," he said to me. "I'm going to help you. I…I'm sorry, I don't know how yet. I don't know. But I am here for you. I'm so proud of you for telling me."

I didn't know what I was supposed to do next. I didn't want to get too far into bonding with Samara's dad because he needed to connect with his daughter, not with me. I hoped he would have the conversation he needed to have with Samara when she was back. I hugged him again.

"Thanks, Dad. I should get to bed."

"Good night. I love you," he responded.

When I got back to Samara's room, she was sitting in the mirror waiting for me. She must have been able to see on my face what had happened.

"You told him," she said, shaking her head and letting her shoulders fall.

"I'm sorry, Samara, but I know it was the right thing to do." I said it even though the sinking feeling in my stomach was making me wonder if that was true. Was it the right thing to do? Should I have given her a chance to tell her dad? No, she never would have. I knew that. But she looked so miserable. I felt awful.

"I hate you." She looked like she meant it. Her eyes were angry, sad, desolate. "We're not switching back tonight. You started this. You deal with my father in the morning. You deal with whatever comes next. Good night."

I wanted to step through the mirror after her, to yell at her and hit her and hold her and apologize to her. But she was gone, so even if I wanted to, I couldn't have. I curled up in Samara's bed, alternately angry and sad and confused and frustrated. And as it turned out, I was wrong. I wasn't out of tears.

chapter 7

How It Should Have Been

Samara

I was so angry at Dee for what she had done. It wasn't her right
or her place to go to my father, to tell him what I had been
doing. If anyone was going to have that conversation, it was
me, and I knew that I could handle the problem without his
help. Or hers. Dee didn't listen when I told her that I hadn't
thought about it all day. And when I got to her school the next
day, all I wanted was to get back at her. At least, I think that
was it.

I found Jamie as quickly as I could. "Hi."

He turned around and looked at me. Nodded to his friends,
took my arm, and walked me over to a corner. "Is it you? I can't
tell who's who anymore."

"It's me," I said. Technically, that wasn't a lie. "I know what you
said to Samara."

Jamie ran a hand over his face. "I'm sorry you had to find out
that way. I didn't mean to say it to her. I meant to say it to you.
I can't believe she told you. I asked her not to. I wanted to tell
you myself." Then he paused. "Wait a minute…you know. Now
you know. Even if I didn't tell you. So? What's, uh, what are you
thinking? What do you think?"

I smiled and tried to look coy. I imagined Dee looking perfectly coy during a conversation like this.

Jamie looked at me strangely. "You don't seem like yourself, Dee."

"I don't feel like myself either. Living on the other side, seeing someone else's life, it made me appreciate my life. It made me appreciate you."

Jamie smiled a little bit, and I remembered that Dee's mom was going to be out that night.

"Mom's working late tonight. Do you want to come over after school?"

"You're sure you're Dee? You seem strange."

I can't believe how well he knows me, I thought. Then I caught myself: *Dee. How well he knows Dee.*

"It's me, I swear. It was just a really long day yesterday, so I'm a little off. I don't know, I guess spending a day being someone else can kinda screw with you. I think that's why...that's why I could really use some company. I don't want to be home alone all night."

The bell rang, and Jamie and I agreed to meet in front of the school at the end of the day.

Kelly seemed to pop up out of nowhere when I left the lunchroom to walk to class, and she took the seat next to me when we got there. She was wearing a miniskirt and an oversized sweatshirt. The sweatshirt was almost longer than the skirt: it was an impressive look. "So, is something going on with you two?" she asked.

"Oh. I don't know what you're talking about," I said.

"You and Jamie? Come on, I saw the way you were looking at each other. Having your quiet little conversation…"

I shrugged, but I was glad that someone had noticed. It meant I hadn't made up that feeling, hadn't made up the way Jamie was looking at me. *Looking at Dee.* That reminder was quieter every time I heard it.

∾

It was going to be hard being Dee with Jamie for the rest of the afternoon. But we didn't talk much on the way back to my place, so at least I had time to prepare.

I went into the apartment first, and even though I knew he had been there before, Jamie still waited in the hall until I invited him in.

"Do you want something to drink?" I asked as he dropped off his stuff in the living room.

"Water's fine."

I brought out two glasses of water and sat on the floor next to him. The shades were open and Jamie was entirely in the sun except for a strip over his chest that was covered by the broken shade that wouldn't stay up. His eyes were clear. He was completely there with me.

He took a sip of his water, "Mmm, liquidy." He smiled and I laughed with him. We sat cross-legged facing each other, and I ran my hand lightly back and forth along the bottom of his leg as he jiggled it up and down slowly.

"So, tell me about yesterday. What's Samara's life like?"

I shook my head a little bit and leaned back from him. I

couldn't believe that Jamie just assumed Dee would tell him all about me. It made me wonder whether any of our conversations had been private. Was Dee sharing everything with Jamie, this guy I hardly knew? Who else was she telling? How many people knew the intimate details of my life? I had trusted her. I had shown her…I wondered if Jamie knew about my mom. About everything that had happened, what I had done to her.

"Oh, it's…umm, it's difficult. She doesn't really have friends or anything. It's kind of sad."

"Sad? Wow. That's not how you usually talk about her."

How would Dee usually talk about me? I never imagined her talking about me at all. I never talk about her. I don't share her secrets with people. I don't talk about her. What would she say when she talked about me? This whole conversation was already making me feel a little light-headed.

"Well it was, umm, you know…It was sad for me. Sad for me to see. You know what I mean." I had to end this conversation; I had to get out of this. "I'm going to go to the bathroom."

I got up and walked into the bathroom, shaking slightly and being sure not to look at the mirror. I wasn't letting Dee through. She wasn't going to ruin this. She had ruined my life; I deserved this at least. I was the one who would have to deal with my father, not her, and now she would have to deal with Jamie.

And the fact that Dee had told Jamie enough about me and my personal life to make him assume that she would just spill her guts about my day, about me, about the things that happened to me, well, that certainly wasn't helping. But Jamie…he was so, he just seemed so…good and sweet. And caring. It wasn't wrong of him to ask; it was wrong of her to say.

I stood in the bathroom for a few minutes and then flushed the toilet. I hoped I would be better at being Dee when I got back.

I sat down next to Jamie again. "Sorry about that. I don't think I'm ready to talk about my alter ego quite yet. Is that okay?"

"Of course it's okay," he said, pushing my hair back from my face. "Anything is okay." He ran his hand along my cheek.

"Listen, Jamie," I tried to sound like Dee. "I don't know if, I mean, tonight might not be the night to…" I trailed off.

"I don't want you to do anything you don't want to do. I…" Jamie started to lean in. "I really care about you." He kissed me. Softly, just for a second.

"Here, hold this," he said and handed me his glass of water. I smiled.

"Wha…" but I trailed off as he put one hand on each side of my face and pulled me close. This time he kissed me harder, longer. He had to know it was me; he had to.

I pushed away a pang of guilt. With everything I was going to have to deal with at home, didn't I deserve this? Didn't I deserve this just once? I didn't plan it to happen the way it did.

Down went the glass of water, most of it down my shirt and the rest onto Jamie's pants. "Oh, my God, I'm so sorry. Oh no! All over you."

"Don't worry about it," he said. Then he smiled. "I handed it to you because I thought *you* wouldn't spill it. I would've too."

"Sorry," I said and bit my lip, starting to lean in again.

Jamie looked at me. "Listen I don't mean to be, umm, but I'm all wet. Do you have pajama pants or something I can change into?"

"Oh, yeah. I'm sorry. Of course." I leaned back for a moment and then stood up. "Let's get out of these wet clothes. Come on, I'll find something in my room. I'm sure there's something you'll fit into." Though he was a lot taller than me and definitely broader.

Jamie followed me to Dee's room. I opened her closet and then turned around and looked at Jamie. "What if, instead…" I went over and kissed him. Jamie ran his hands up and down my back, then under the back of my shirt and forward over my stomach. I put my arms up, and he pulled my shirt over my head. I ran my hands over his chest, down over his abs, and began to unbutton his pants. I slid them down.

The way Jamie was touching me, the way he looked at me… I felt like a virgin again. This was how it should have been the first time. Not forced, not manipulated into it. This was how it was supposed to be. I felt Jamie start walking me backward slowly, carefully. I sat down and felt Jamie turn me onto the bed. His hand slid to my back, and he unhooked my bra. It felt so right having him there lying next to me.

He rolled backward for a second and looked at me, first into my eyes, then down my body. "Your body…" Jamie ran his hands over my arms, Dee's arms, Dee's body. "It's so perfect." He pulled a sheet over us and rolled back toward me, pulling me into him. He dropped his voice to a whisper. "Look."

"What?" I asked.

"We're naked together."

I smiled at him, pulled my arm out, looked into his eyes, and stroked his cheek with my index finger. "I know."

He leaned in and kissed me again, holding me against him. He kissed my lips, my cheek, my neck, and then paused for a second and whispered, "Do you want to make love?"

"Yes."

"This will be your first time, won't it? It's okay to say—"

I cut him off. "I know. I said yes."

And we did. I'd never made love before. With tenderness and care and knowing that he would be there after it happened. Knowing that if I had said no, he would have still wrapped his arms around me just the same way. And held me and looked at me, and…

∽

Afterward, as Jamie rolled me over and put his arms around me, he pulled me close and whispered to me, "This right here, this is the best part." His left arm under my head, he clasped my right hand in his, intertwining our fingers.

"I'm happy," I said to him. And it was true.

I heard the front door close.

"Lorna? Sweetheart, are you home?"

"Oh shit! She wasn't supposed to be home for hours!" I said to him.

Jamie's eyes widened.

"Go!" I hissed.

Jamie got up and started hopping around the room, pulling his wet jeans back on and then his socks. I knew it wasn't funny, that

I should have been helping, but I laughed. He looked ridiculous hopping around my room with one sock on.

"Coming, Mom. Just finishing up a…a paper and don't want to lose my train of thought. Just a minute."

"I'm starting dinner," she called.

I threw the window open as Jamie pulled his shirt over his head. "Take the fire escape," I said.

With one leg out the window, Jamie turned back to me. "Come here."

I walked over. He grabbed the back of my head and pulled me into him, kissing me hard. "That was amazing. You," he kissed me, "are," again, "incredible."

And out the window he went.

I closed the window and walked toward the kitchen on wobbly legs. He was right: that was amazing. It was…better than amazing.

"Hi, Mom. You're home early. Good day?"

chapter 8

Step Back and Try Again

Dee

It was the right thing to do. Wasn't it? I knew her dad had to know. That was the only way she would get the help she needed.

I wanted to do something for Samara that she would have trouble doing herself. Samara might be good with boys, but I'm good with girls. I wanted to win her friends back. Win Eva back at least…she had already said I had nice hair. And the rest of the group would follow if she did.

I wanted school to become a place Samara enjoyed, where she went to see her friends. I mean, I spent a lot of my day thinking about Samara, but I still had friends at school. I like school. I always have. And I felt like Samara was missing that.

I spent the whole next morning in school psyching myself up for sitting with Eva at lunch. I didn't think she and Samara were friends, but she was the only person who had even spoken to me, spoken to *Samara* the previous day, and I knew I had to start somewhere.

I went to the bathroom before lunch, hoping in vain that Samara would be there, that she would have some advice for me, even if she wasn't ready to switch back. But she wasn't. I took a deep breath and walked into the lunchroom. It took me a minute to find Eva's table.

"Hi, Eva. Hi, everyone. Umm, can I join you?"

There was a pause for what felt like an hour and a half, even though it was probably only a few seconds until Eva piped up. "Of course. Tommy, scoot down."

"Why the sudden compulsion for company?" Tommy asked, looking at me and imperceptibly shaking his head.

"Tommy," Eva said quietly, tilting her head to one side.

"No, it's okay," I said. "I've just been doing some thinking, and I miss you guys."

"Miss us?" asked a girl at the other end of the table. "We were never—" but Eva caught her eye and she stopped.

"So," Eva said, pulling everyone's eyes back to her, "how did everyone do on that chem test? Tough stuff."

"I know I bombed it," said one guy who I didn't recognize.

I zoned out, thinking about Samara, and forcing myself to laugh when I heard everyone else laughing. I reminded myself to thank Eva later for getting the focus off me. From the discussion about the test, they moved on to the dance that had been a week before and a party that one of the girls was having that weekend. Eva quickly said to me that I was welcome to come if I wasn't busy. I smiled and thanked the girl who was throwing the party. I'd have to remember to tell Samara.

After that I had trouble focusing on what people were saying. I noticed that the cafeteria smelled the way school lunchrooms always smell: horrible, even though the food isn't that bad. It's just standard cafeteria food. Why *does* it smell so bad all the time?

The food they served really didn't look bad, and it hardly tasted like anything, just bland. It was just the smell and the fluorescent lighting that made the whole room look like a hospital and made everyone in it look a little bit grayer, a little bit paler, and a little bit sicklier than they would the rest of the time.

I tried to make myself listen to the conversations, but I couldn't make myself interested in people I didn't know and tests I hadn't taken. At the end of lunch, I really wanted to talk to Eva, so I went out of my way to linger. After everyone else had left, I put my hand mirror back into my bag and slowly stood up again.

"Eva?"

"Yeah?"

"I need to talk to you. I…I need to tell you something. Today at lunch, I mean, and yesterday, I just wanted to say that, well, I don't even remember what happened between the two of us. I don't even know why we're not friends anymore, and I miss you. I meant that when I said it before. I want to be friends again. Do you think that would be possible? I'm turning over a new leaf, trying to be a whole new person."

"Oh, Samara. Look, I've missed you too. And, I don't know, maybe you really are trying to turn over a new leaf. But you're still you, like it or not. We can try, I guess. I mean we can definitely try. But, well, I was pretty hurt when you stopped talking to me. And I don't know if I can truly forgive that. Not overnight at least." She stood up and walked out of the lunchroom, and I looked around and felt alone. Completely alone.

∾

When I got home that night, Samara's dad was already there waiting. He was sitting at the kitchen table, hands folded on top of the table in front of him. He looked at his thumbs, at the table, at the wall behind me, even up at the ceiling. He did everything but look at me.

"All right," he said, beginning to twiddle his thumbs slowly. Right over left, left over right, right over left. Very slowly. I waited. He continued, pronouncing each syllable in a hard tone, using each word as its own complete thought. "I've decided…what I want to do." Right over left. "This is…what is going to be best for you." Left over right. He paused to raise his eyebrows at the cookbooks on the bookshelf. I guess the cookbooks didn't have any questions, so he went on. "There's a place…in Florida…that helps girls when they're in trouble. Depressed, or you know…"

Rehab. He was going to send Samara to rehab.

"They only take girls for a week at a time because of the high demand. There is usually a long waiting list, but I called some people and they can take you right away. You need to be there Monday."

He unclasped his hands and held onto the table instead as if preparing for me to yell and kick and scream. As if the table would be able to stop a huge wind from blowing him away. He had rehearsed talking to me. He had prepared for what he thought my responses should have been.

He had no idea what I would be thinking right now, no idea what *Samara* would be thinking right now. *I* had no idea what Samara would be thinking right now. I was almost glad I was still here. At least I would be able to break the news to Samara instead of her hearing this ridiculous semi-talk her father was giving. That was something.

"Then after that," he continued, "you're going to have a weekly support group. The people at the…facility…will help you find one you're comfortable with." His body wilted and he looked so old. "This is okay. We're going to get through this. You and me. You're going to be fine. We're going to be fine." The cookbooks clearly appreciated his moral support.

I had nothing to say. I was in shock. I couldn't begin to imagine how Samara would or should respond to all of this. I couldn't respond, and eventually he just said something about letting me think it over for a few minutes. He got up, kissed the top of my head, and squeezed my shoulder. I winced.

I spent the next day wondering how I was going to tell Samara that she had to go to rehab. She was not the type to just open up to a bunch of people she didn't know, and I couldn't imagine her going to a weekly support group.

By the end of the day, I was thrilled to get back to my locker. It was cold for early December, but it took me a few minutes to bundle up—longer than usual because I accidentally put on my gloves before zipping up my coat. That gave Eva enough time to come and find me.

"Okay, look. Maybe you are turning over a new leaf. You've seemed happier. I like that you're happier. And…I *have* missed you. We used to be so close before…you know."

"I don't. I honestly don't remember anymore," I said, pulling on my hat and then my gloves again. I took a quick look in the mirror in Samara's locker but nothing. I turned to look at Eva again.

"I just meant…" She lowered her voice. "Before your mom died."

"Oh. Well, I'm obviously not going to say I'm over that. But I am trying to be me again. I'm trying to…I don't know. I think I need help, though. I need you guys again. I need my friends."

"Well, I guess I can try to be here for you. I'm sorry to be so blunt, but if you're going to…to, like, flip-flop again, I don't know if I can handle that. Well, actually, I know I can't."

"I'm trying. Please believe me."

"I'm trying to believe you."

It hadn't occurred to me that Samara could stop me from getting into my own world, but as it turned out, she could. I had to wait in front of the mirror in Samara's room for most of the night. I was glad it was Friday. I occupied myself by returning all of the things in Samara's room to where they belonged. I knew Samara would be upset if she found out I had gone through all of her stuff.

I looked at the dolls, the dresses, the notebooks. I turned them all over in my hands and put them back in the cupboard. Then I got to the razor. I knew it was easy to get another one—to get a knife, to get anything—but I wrapped it in a tissue and threw the razor away, hoping that I would be able to stop Samara just one time, just one day. I wanted to make her think about what she was doing. Think about not doing it.

I would try to get through the mirror every few minutes, but each time I ended up in the black box between worlds and I had to step back and try again. The fifth time, I stood silently in the black box for a long time. I wanted to see if my eyes could adjust to the darkness and I could find my way around without touching anything. But nothing happened as I stood there.

I tried to blink my eyes, move my head, clench my face, but I felt like my whole body wasn't there unless I was touching the sides of the box. My soul stepped through the mirror. My body was left behind. I supposed that was why Samara and I took each other's bodies when stepping through.

Then I began to feel the same tingling I had felt when Samara and I had switched bodies for the first time. A moment later, I found myself back in my own body, in my own room, on my own carpet, looking at Samara through the mirror in front of me.

"Lorna," she said, nodding her head coldly.

"Samara, don't be angry at me. Please, don't be like this. We… we need each other."

But even as I said it, I knew it wasn't true. I was tired of it. I was tired of her blaming me for everything I had done for her. I had seen her suffering and tried to help. I had found her and befriended her and switched places with her and given her a chance to see another world and another life, and I was so tired of her acting like this.

"You know what? Whatever. Be angry at me. You want to blame me for all your problems? Fine. But at least listen to what I have to say. Before you talk to your dad, there's something you should know—"

"No, Dee, there are some things *I* have to tell *you*," she said.

"I'll take care of whatever it is, Samara. I can take care of myself. Now listen to me."

"What? As if I need your help to take care of myself? Bullshit, Dee."

"That's not what I was trying to say." But it *was* what I was trying to say.

"My dad's calling me. You can fill me in on the fascinating things that went on in my life while I was away some other time. Oh, and if I were you, I'd go talk to Jamie. You have plenty to talk about." Then she walked away and I was left with the empty reflection across from me.

I stared at my room and then closed my eyes, feeling momentarily relieved to be home, to be back where I belonged. Then Samara's smirk in the mirror flashed in front of me again. I realized that she was not that good an actor, and I ran out of my room to go find Jamie. I needed to know what it was *now*. Right away.

"Lorna, where are you—" Mom must have just gotten in from work. She was cooking dinner, and I felt bad that I had to go and couldn't help her get anything ready. She looked so tired. Days on end on her feet can do that, I suppose.

"Sorry, Mom. No time to explain. I need to—" but I cut myself off to go give her a hug. I had always appreciated my mom, but after seeing Samara's dad, I appreciated her more than ever.

"Hey, sweetheart." She kissed the top of my head. "What's going on? You've been just…off for the last few days. Stay, talk to me."

"I can't. Over dinner, definitely. But I really need to talk to someone right now."

"Yes, you do. Your mother. Sit down, sweetheart. Keep me company while I cook. What's going on? Is this person you *have* to talk to a certain boy? Who slipped out the window when I came home?"

"What?" Samara had screwed things up so much worse than I had thought. "No. I mean, maybe? No. Please, Mom. I need to find him and figure things out."

She put a hand on my shoulder. "Lorna, it might be better to figure things out before you find him."

She looked me straight in the eye, and it felt like a standoff. I knew that she was right. But I didn't have enough clues to figure things out yet. There was a knock on the door. We stared for a moment before I ducked under her arm to answer it.

Jamie.

"Hi."

I looked imploringly at my mother. Jamie looked nervously at the floor, tapping one foot rapidly as we waited together for my mom's decision. My mother shook her head at me and sighed. "Think about what I just said."

"Please, Mom."

"Fine. Go. It's your choice. Take a sweater. And I'm holding you to that real-conversation-over-dinner promise. This isn't over."

"Thank you, Mom," I said and ran in for a second to give her a hug. A real hug.

Jamie waited until we got outside to turn to me and say, "We have to talk."

chapter 9

Feeling Defeated

Samara

I looked at Dee in the mirror and thought, *We're back*. I heard my father calling me, and I wondered what he was doing home so early on a Friday.

"Samara, can you come down here for a minute?" I went downstairs and stopped on the landing, looking down at him. He had one hand on the banister and a foot on the first step. "I wanted to give you this…" He held a pamphlet toward me. "And to see if you started packing already, if there's anything you need…"

"Packing? Packing for what? Where are we going?" I walked down the stairs and reached out to take the pamphlet he was holding. It took a moment to sink in. *Reality Rehabilitation*. I opened it and stared at the inside. It was filled with text, but I didn't understand any of it.

"Rehab? I'm supposed to be…I'm supposed to be packing for rehab?"

"We talked about it, honey. It's only for a week. To help you deal with…help us deal with…" his voice trailed off.

I felt a small flame begin in my stomach, come up through my intestines, and burn out the back of my throat and the roof of my mouth. I was sure that when I opened my mouth I would breathe out fire, but instead I screamed, "I am not going to rehab!"

My father took a step back, and I looked down at him from three stairs up. "Samara, you...you said it was a good idea. We talked about this," he repeated meekly.

"I must've been out of my fucking mind. There's no way I'm going."

"Yes, you are. This is not your decision. This is what's best for you, and it's not your decision."

"To hell it's not," I said. I ran down the stairs and stomped out of the house, unsure where I was going.

❧

I found myself outside the cemetery where my mother was buried. I had never been to visit before, though Dad had pointed out the grave when we drove by the cemetery once. I hadn't even been to her funeral. My father had told me that it would be too much for me to handle, and I guess it would have been.

The man at the gate of the cemetery asked if I wanted to buy flowers. I shook my head and put my hand on the gate in front of me. All I needed to do was push it open and walk in and ask my mom for help. But I couldn't. I had never been able to go in, not since she died.

The man with the flowers continued pushing me to buy, and finally I crossed the street to get away from him. I went to a park and sat down on a bench.

When Mom died, instead of letting me mourn, my dad had told me to write letters to her.

"It's better than crying," he told me. "Write down everything you wish you could tell her. Then give them to me, and I'll send them to her so when you get to heaven, she'll be all caught up. It will be like she was here all the time."

I wrote letters for years, giving them to my father in sealed envelopes addressed:

My Mommy
the Most Beautiful House
Heaven, the Sky

After I had stopped writing, when I got old enough to realize the letters were never being sent, that there was no heaven, that I wasn't going to see my mom again and she wasn't going to see me again, I went into my dad's room while he was out. I went through his sock drawer and his closet and eventually found them all on the back of a shelf tied up with a red ribbon. I moved them into my room, but I was never able to bring myself to reread them. What had my life become since she died?

Sitting on that park bench, I wondered for the first time in a long time what I had written, what I had told her. I realized how cold I was. I had stormed out without thinking about where I was going or the fact that I might like a jacket when I got there. I looked around and wasn't surprised that there wasn't anybody else in the park. In the few days since I had left, it had gone from fall to winter; the trees were barer than they were orange or red. I got up and slowly walked home. I sneaked in as quietly as I could and tiptoed up the stairs.

I closed the door of my room and opened the third dresser drawer. There, underneath my sweaters, was a stack of envelopes tied with a red ribbon. I sat on the floor with my legs crossed and stared at the stack for a moment. I untied them and ripped open the one on top.

Dear Mom,

Since I last wrote to you, I've started seeing somebody new. I like him. More than the last one, at least. I don't know if you would approve. I don't think so. A few weeks ago, I got drunk with him. It felt good. For one night, I wasn't thinking about you. Everyone else doesn't think about you all the time, but the only time I don't think about you is when I'm distracted. Then at night when I'm alone in bed, every moment that I didn't think about you makes me feel guilty. I don't want to feel bad. Not like this. It's…it's too hard. So now I sometimes get drunk before I go to bed.

One year ago today, I came home from school and I wanted to show you a report I had done well on. One year ago today, I had to see your empty eyes that didn't love me anymore. One year ago today, I cried while I was lying in bed by myself and Dad was downstairs making "arrangements."

One year ago today, I had to tell my friends that I didn't have a mother anymore. One year ago today, you left me. Alone. To figure things out.

So today I figured things out. Today I thought the less I can think about you, the better. Today I decided I want to do things without wondering if you would tell me they were okay. Today I cried alone in bed when I woke up and then cried alone in the shower. Today I am crying alone in my room while I write you a letter.

But tomorrow I will not cry anymore. Tomorrow I will not think about you at school or on my way home. Tomorrow I will not write you another letter. Tomorrow I will do anything it takes to not worry about you. Tomorrow I will think of a way to make things better. Tomorrow I will not tell you things that will upset you.

I hope you don't miss me as much as I miss you.

Your baby girl,

Samara

I reread the letter and remembered why I had stopped writing the letters. While I was sitting in the park, I had thought it was because I'd stopped believing she would receive them. But in my room, rereading the letter a third time, I realized it was because I was embarrassed. I was ashamed of what I was doing, so ashamed that I couldn't even tell my mother about it in a letter she would never receive.

I looked at my arms and felt the cuts burn as my tears fell on them. I would have been thirteen when I wrote that last letter. And already, I had been acting older than I should have.

I sneaked back down the stairs into the front of the house and slammed the front door. My father came out when he heard the noise.

"I know that this is hard for you," he said as he walked in, "but I'm your father and I know what's best for you."

"No, Dad," I said, shaking my head. "I don't care what I said last week." What had Dee said last week? "I'm not going to rehab. I don't need it. And I'm not going."

But three days later, I found myself on a plane to Florida.

I spent most of the trip wondering how Dee's conversation with Jamie had gone and if he *had* known it was me the whole time. If it brought the two of them closer or pushed them farther apart. I wondered for a moment if Dee had sent me to this place, had agreed to this, just to get me away. But angry as I was at her, I didn't think that was Dee. And she hadn't known about Jamie when she had told my dad.

As the cab drove up to the…institution, I guess…I couldn't help but think it seemed dank and gross. It was brighter inside, but the trees outside did very little to cheer up the concrete exterior. There were windows, but they were barred like a prison. There was a courtyard in the center of the building that was filled with flowers. But I couldn't see that from the outside. I shuddered.

A nurse met me outside and smiled. "Welcome."

She walked me in and down a long hallway. It was brightly lit, but something about the whole place still felt depressing. Which was strange because this place was supposed to be able to cure me of sadness. Or anger. Or something.

"This is your room. Your roommate hasn't arrived yet, but she's on her way. Her name is Sasha. I'm sure the two of you will get along fine." I looked in. The room had flowered wallpaper and two made beds. I watched the nurse out of the corner of my eye. She was still smiling in a weird, fake way. I turned around and looked at her straight on.

"Something else?"

She continued smiling, unfazed. "I'll let you get settled for a few minutes. Come on out when you're done." I moved in after her and began to close the door.

"Open, please," she said, smiling. I nodded, already feeling defeated, and dropped my backpack on the bed. I walked around the room, looked out the window and tapped on it. Plexiglas. I went into the bathroom. No mirror. No way out. I walked around and found a nurse to ask about it.

"Mirrors encourage focusing on our outer image. We want to see what's inside," one of the always smiling nurses told me when I asked. They took girls with all sorts of problems, and I think the lack of mirrors was mostly for the girls with serious eating disorders. But I guess the reason was supposed to be overarching.

When I got back, Sasha was there unpacking. At first, she refused to tell me why she was there, but later in the week she admitted to me that she had tried to kill herself a number of times. That didn't seem to be the most immediate reason. But she wouldn't say what the trigger was that had brought her here this time.

Once she finished unpacking, she just sat on her bed curled up, watching me unpack. She didn't have much with her. I guess I brought more than I needed, but how do you pack for rehab? About half of what I had stayed in my suitcase the whole week, but while I unpacked the first night, I could feel Sasha's eyes on my back.

"First time?"

"What?" I asked her.

"Is it your first time in a…in a place like this? In a hospital?"

"Yeah. My dad sent me. What about you?"

She smiled ironically. "Before I came, I sat down to figure out exactly how much time I've spent inpatient this year. I've spent more time in a hospital this year than I have at home."

I stopped unpacking and sat down on my bed to really look at her. She was pretty, but she was so thin that she looked gaunt. She had this look…this sad look, like the one my mom used to have when she thought no one was watching. Sasha had dark brown eyes that seemed like they sunk into her head further than other people's. Her hair was wispy and thin. She seemed to melt as I looked at her. She stared back at me, hardly blinking.

"Does it help?" I asked finally.

"I think it would help if I could be in a hospital all the time. But otherwise, I mean, for a little while. I guess. I don't know…I get home and it feels like everything just comes back." I nodded. She pursed her lips for a moment. "It won't help you if you don't want it to," she said.

I wondered if I did want it to. I wanted to stop cutting. I wanted to stop feeling this way all the time. In a way, I knew it was good that the hospital had taken everything away from me. I wasn't sure that deciding I wasn't going to do it was going to be enough. Maybe I did need the help. Or at least the friendship. But on the other hand…well, I already knew I wasn't going to cut myself anymore. If I could get through the hellish week ahead of me, maybe I could try for change. Try to make things be different when I got home.

We were given the first day to get to know each other. My roommate recognized about a quarter of the girls there, and they immediately formed a group of "frequent visitors." Sasha invited me to join them and I tried sitting with them for a little while, but they were swapping stories about what had happened since they were last institutionalized…I guess they had found their community. Most of them were part of an online support group where they were able to stay in touch and try to keep each other out, keep each other clean. Or whatever the equivalent is when you're depressed.

"I thought I was doing really well," said one girl. "I decided to go off my meds because I was tired of that…that flat feeling." There was general nodding. "I did okay for a couple of weeks, but…" She trailed off and gestured to where we were. In the over-flowered garden of a cement hospital.

I didn't quite fit. Apparently, I was old for my first visit, at least according to these girls, and I wasn't really ready to talk to them about what I had gone through.

On the second day, I spoke to one of the psychiatrists for a short while and then to a nurse for most of the afternoon. She asked if I had made friends with the other girls, and I told her I hadn't. Sasha was nice, but she wasn't a friend. I mean, we probably wouldn't have even talked if we hadn't coincidentally been in the same room.

"Sometimes, it can help to talk to other people who are going through the same thing," the nurse said, inclining her head slightly to the side. "You shouldn't count on someone else for your recovery, of course, but it can help. That's why we have this secluded location. Build a support group for yourself. You can stay in touch if you choose to afterward. And if not, there are groups you can join when you get home."

"I'm not really ready to tell a bunch of girls who are trying to kill themselves that my mom succeeded." Plus, I thought to myself, I don't think telling them I slept with my reflection's boyfriend would go over too well. Ever since I'd arrived, I had been worrying about someone finding out why I was really there, finding out about Dee, and claiming I was schizo or something.

I looked at the nurse and almost felt bad for her. She was forced to keep a smile plastered on her face all day, and I tried to focus on what she was saying, instead of on the abnormally chipper way she was saying it. I wondered if she was a rehab graduate. If I felt like I was stuck here forever, what must she feel like? I mean, I would only be there for a week.

On the fourth day, my psychiatrist asked why I think I cut myself. I was getting frustrated with this question and answered the same way I had for the first three days. "I stopped cutting myself." I hadn't cut myself since I was Dee.

"I know this is hard, but I also know that's not true. Those are some pretty new scars," she said, pointing at my arms. "It might help if you picked up another hobby, something else you can do with your hands maybe."

"What sort of hobby? So far, I haven't found a hobby I actually enjoy that's legal."

"What do you like to do? What do you do for fun?"

It was a good question. What did I do for fun? What had I done before Dee and I started spending all our spare time together? "I...design doll clothes?"

"Do you?" she asked, smiling in a way that looked slightly more genuine for a moment.

"Well, I used to. I haven't in a long time. Not since my mom died really. But I think I was okay at it when I was little. My mom and I used to make clothes for my dolls and stuff."

She smiled. "Have you considered picking it up again?"

I could try. I hadn't even thought of designing in years. But I used to do it all the time when I was little. "I'll try." True answers were the easiest answers to give.

By the last day, I had found a couple of girls I could talk to. They were other first-timers and each had her own problems. But it did kind of help to hear that other people were going through something similar. That I didn't have to be alone in this. I did more listening than talking, but I guess hearing the other girls talk was a reminder that I wasn't the only one with problems.

Everybody was dealing with something—pain, divorce, eating disorders…I wasn't the only one here for a reason. Or no reason. Sometimes people just hurt. I didn't feel like I needed this help. I was already taking care of myself, so I didn't need all of these doctors and nurses. I told Sasha that my dad was making me go to a support group when I got home.

"That's good," she said. "You should go. It helps."

"But I don't need it," I argued with her. "I'm cured. I'm done. It's just going to be a reminder that I was sick."

"You don't just get 'cured.' It's more complicated than that. Just deciding that everything will be fine doesn't necessarily make everything fine." The doctor had said the same thing, but I hadn't really believed her. Hearing Sasha say it helped convince me.

"I think I can handle it. I have some support. I have the support of—" but I stopped myself short. All this time, somewhere in the back of my mind I had thought I would have Jamie and Dee when I got home. Jamie wasn't in my world. I didn't have his support. He didn't even know me. And I didn't think that Dee and I would be speaking when I got back. I wasn't over her sending me here. And as much as my dad would try, he always had trouble supporting me when I needed it most. Despite the fact that I stopped mid-sentence, Sasha knew where I was going.

"I've been through this, and I'm never going to get out of it. I've been here for too long." She moved to my bed and put her hand on my knee. "But you have a good chance. Don't leave your recovery to one other person, especially a boyfriend. It's as unfair to him as it is to you. You don't want to trap him."

"I don't have a boyfriend," I snapped. More honest words, but I immediately felt bad. She had been more helpful than anyone else while I was here. I couldn't tell her what was really going on, obviously, but I didn't mean to go so hot and cold on her all week the way I had. She moved back to her bed, and I was so unsure what to say that I couldn't even look at her. I turned around and went back to packing. I heard the door close and knew she had already left the room.

❧

When they drove us to the airport to leave, the nurses all hugged us good-bye, as though their smiles were anything more than plaster, and offered to talk to us if we ever needed them. Sasha hugged me right before I got on a plane to go home. She whispered, "Seriously, you don't have to do this alone. Get the help. You need it more than you think."

I nodded. She knew. She knew much better than I did.

A part of me knew that being there had helped. That I had gotten better. But another—bigger—part of me felt that rehab was something I would never be able to overcome. I would always know I'd been institutionalized. I was haunted by the experiences of the people around me, by the papered walls and the feeling that those helping me already saw me as less than them. They already saw me as crazy, as a forever patient who would be in and out my whole life, the way Sasha was. I didn't want that to happen to me.

When I saw my father, the anger and the frustration rekindled. And all the good the trip had done me floated away into the night. All I could think was that he was picking up his daughter from her trip to an *institution*.

"Welcome home," he said, moving to hug me. I stepped back.

"If you ever make me do something like that again, I will never come back. I'm not just your crazy daughter that you can ship off when I get too complicated. You deal with me, or I don't deal with you. You're my dad. You don't just get to pick and choose what in my life to be a part of."

We didn't talk on the ride home.

chapter 10

Smack in the Face

Dee

We were more than halfway down the block, and still Jamie hadn't said anything. I desperately needed to know what happened with Samara, and eventually I got tired of waiting.

"Look, Jamie, about what happened—"

"That's what I wanted to talk to you about. Are you…" He paused, taking my hand as we continued walking. "Are you okay?" He stopped and took my other hand, curling our fingers together, turning me toward him. "I know I wanted this. You did too, right?" I smiled at the way he looked at me, and he leaned in and kissed me softly, and I felt my knees shake and my mind go blank for a moment.

What had happened with Samara? And why did I get the feeling he thought it was *me* we were talking about? Samara must have told him that I liked him, but what else had happened? This felt natural, which was amazing. It was even more than I expected. But something about it was too easy, too simple.

"I'm happy too." I let go of his hand and we kept walking. "But I'm a little bit…confused," I said.

"After we…you know. I thought it was pretty clear what was happening. I didn't think you would've if we weren't together.

I thought it was amazing. We're working, aren't we? I mean, doesn't it feel right?"

He put his arm around me as we walked, and it was true. It did feel right. It felt...perfect. But this perfection wasn't achieved with me. It was achieved with Samara. This whole thing had gone so wrong. But at that moment, it did feel so right. Then a terrifying thought occurred to me. Maybe Jamie thought I was Samara. Had he said my name? I tried to replay our conversation in my head. I was pretty sure he had said my name. He had; I was sure he had. So he had to know it was me.

"Jamie, what—" But he cut me off.

"I feel like I got cheated out of holding you after. I didn't want to just leave you that way. I didn't mean to just run out. When your mom came home, I got scared. But I didn't want you to think...I didn't want you to think I don't want to be with you."

"Holding me, holding me after..."

"After, you know..." He seemed embarrassed for a moment. I was trying desperately to fit the pieces together, to figure out what he was trying to tell me. He didn't seem to know that Samara and I had switched back. I wondered if he knew we had switched places at all. After what? My head was in such a fog that I was so confused about what he was talking about. "I feel like you're not here with me," he said.

"Sorry, I'm just...like I said. I'm just confused."

"You're not...rethinking this, are you? You don't regret it?"

"I don't regret..." It hit me smack in the face. My mom said he had slipped out the window when she came home. Samara had a look in her eye I had never seen before. He kept avoiding saying what "it" was. Jamie was apologizing for not holding me "after." We had had sex. Or Jamie thought we had. He and Samara had. What the hell had Samara done? Why, why had she done this?

"Oh, my God, did we...? I have to...I have to go. I'm sorry. I—" I searched for an excuse. "I promised my mom I'd come home as quickly as possible." I turned to walk home.

"Wait, but Dee—"

"Sorry," I said, pulling my arm away from him.

"What's the matter? Are we okay?"

"Yeah, we're...we're fine, Jamie." He pulled me toward him and kissed me again. It didn't feel right anymore. I wanted to get him off me. This was making my stomach churn. When he let me go, I turned and walked home as quickly as I could. That kiss wasn't mine. It was Samara's.

When I walked in, my mom was sitting at the table, quickly flipping the pages of a magazine. She looked up at me when I walked in. "Everything okay?"

"Yeah, I...I think so. Thanks. I just needed to talk to him."

"Well," she said, "now that that's sorted out. My turn. What's going on? What happened to that girl who told me everything? The one who didn't keep secrets from her mom?"

"She...she went on a little vacation. I'm so sorry, Mom. It's me now, though. I'm back. I'm so sorry about everything. I won't lie to you."

My mom never got mad at me. I couldn't believe that Samara had been able to alienate her. I didn't think my expectations of

Samara had been that high: just don't actively destroy my relationships with the people who care about me. She had to have done this all on purpose. I would never have believed she could do it if the evidence wasn't sitting right in front of me.

"When I came home, it was Jamie slipping out your window, wasn't it? That was the noise I heard? The shuffling around in your room?"

"It…" I couldn't lie to her; I just promised her I wouldn't. "It was. I'm sorry, Mom. I should have talked to you about this before. I shouldn't have. But Mom, I like him. I really like him. And, he likes me too. I think…I think he loves me, Mom."

She sighed. "It's okay, sweetheart. It's okay. You're growing up. I knew it would happen sometime." She smiled for the first time. "As long as you're careful, as long as you're safe. You're right, though, you should have talked to me about it. Do you really think you were ready? Are the two of you even together?"

"Yeah, we are. But I don't know." I finally sat down at the table with her. "I don't know how this happened. I didn't plan it. Not like this." Everything I was saying was true—this was *certainly* not in my plans. My mom would never know how true that was, but it felt good to be able to talk to her. I had missed her so much while I was away.

"It's okay, sweetheart. It's…it's time for your first love. I just wish…I wish you looked happier right now."

"I'm just conflicted, I guess."

My mom got up and walked over to me. She leaned down and put her arms around me. "I'm here if you need me."

I felt the tears start, and as much as I tried to contain them, they kept coming. I wished I could tell my mom what I was really crying about. I wished I could tell her that I had a new best friend who was hurting—and who was hurting me. That I thought I could help her. That I had trusted her. But I had just made things worse. And so had she. That we had both screwed up so badly.

I spent most of the weekend curled up in bed, trying to figure out what had happened. How had Samara and I gotten ourselves here? How had she and Jamie gotten themselves there? I couldn't tell left from right anymore. I couldn't tell what I wanted.

༄

When I got back to school on Monday, I began checking the mirror constantly for Samara. I figured if nothing else, she'd get angry and come to yell at me. But she didn't. When I hadn't heard from or seen her by Friday, I was getting really concerned. I started keeping a small mirror on my desk in every class. My friend Kelly kept shooting me strange looks about it.

"What's that about?" she finally asked on Day Two.

I had been waiting for this question. And I was prepared for it. "I watched this totally creepy movie the other day where this guy strangles his ex-girlfriend by sneaking up behind her. This way, I can be sure that won't happen."

She started laughing and I bit my lip. Would it work? I had practiced the excuse over and over (in the mirror, of course) as soon as Kelly started looking at me strangely. "Oh, come on," I said, "haven't you ever been completely terrified after a movie?"

She wasn't laughing at me anymore, but instead looking at me skeptically. "Who do you think is going to kill you in school? What movie was this? Jeez."

I smiled and shrugged a little, hoping that would answer her questions.

No matter how much time I spent staring in the mirror, though, Samara never appeared.

And the week had been a slow one. I barely knew what was going on with the people around me, and it was hard to tell who Samara had isolated and who she had made friends with. Clearly, Jamie's friends thought we were closer than I was used to, but I wasn't sure about anyone else.

Jamie walked me home on Tuesday, and as we started up my block, he put his arm around me and said, "I like us."

"I like us too?" I said but my voice went up at the end of my sentence, something my mother constantly warned me about.

"But?"

"But what are we exactly? I mean, you said we were together, right? So what does that mean?"

"I...I kind of assumed that you were my girlfriend."

I smiled. "So you're my boyfriend?"

Jamie kissed me. I took that to be a yes. And the kiss felt like mine. Like he was mine.

∽

I caught up with Samara just as I was about to leave the mirror Sunday night.

"Samara! Finally! Where have you been?" She turned toward

125

me slowly, and I could see the dark bags under her eyes. I could see that she had withdrawn over the week. She seemed limp.

She looked me up and down and then looked away. "I wasn't allowed to have a mirror at rehab."

"Well, what was it like? How was it? How do you feel?"

"Oh, wonderful. I'm all cured," she said sarcastically. "Thanks, Dee. You obviously know what's best for me. I can't believe I ever doubted you."

"Samara, don't be like that."

"You sent me away, Dee. What do you want from me? You expect me to thank you? Fuck you. You made this mess of my life and you left. And now I will forever be stamped as someone who was in a mental institution. And what about what you did with the kids at school? People I don't like are trying to coax conversation out of me."

"Who? What are you talking about? Eva? She's perfectly nice. I don't know what your problem with her is," I said. Samara was so dramatic about everything. Everyone was evil; everyone was out to get her.

"You don't know anything about my problems, Dee. You really want to know why I don't like Eva?"

"I really do," I said, crossing my arms and taking a step back.

"She left me, Dee. My mom committed suicide. I needed friends. And she abandoned me. She decided it was *just too hard on her*. I heard her telling someone else in the bathroom. If she thought it was hard on her, what did she think was happening to me? What was I asking of her? Besides someone to listen when I talked. I thought I'd found that in you, but I guess we can both see that that isn't true.

"And who are *you* to decide who I should be friends with anyway? You're the one who tells me I deserve more? Well, believe me, Dee, these girls are not more. They're the kinds of friends who disappear when things get hard."

I was so tired of Samara's blame-it-on-the-world attitude. She was blaming me for not being a friend? She'd had sex with the guy I liked. She'd had sex with her best friend's boyfriend. Who was she to define friendship?

"You know what, Samara? Maybe it was hard on her. Maybe you're not, like, the easiest person in the world to deal with. Ever think of that? What, you think your life is so hard and the rest of us have it so easy all the time? Fuck that. If someone wants to be your friend, why don't you just let them?"

She just shook her head at me and walked away.

chapter 11

Industrial-Strength Cleaner

Samara

I was glad to get out of the car, glad to get out of the drive away from rehab, glad to be rid of that week of my life. It had snowed while I was away, and it was freezing compared to Florida. I went straight up to my room and lay down on the floor. The room smelled different. It smelled like Dee and like hospital cleaning products. The exact smell I was trying to get away from. I heard my father knock. He pushed the door open without waiting for a response. I sat up and put my arms around my knees.

"I had your room cleaned while you were away," he said, looking around. That explained the smell. I thought being away from the hospital would let me get *away* from the hospital. It was funny: not even industrial-strength cleaners could get the smell of Dee out of my room. I looked up at my dad, and he finished staring around the room and looked down at me, finally kneeling down so we were at eye level.

"I have something for you," he said.

"What?"

He handed me a notebook and a pen. I looked at them and back at him. "What's this for?"

"In case you need to write down what you're feeling. Or draw or something."

"Oh. Well, thanks, Dad. Great."

"Okay. Well. I'll let you get settled in and unpack." He stood up again. "I'll be in my room if you need anything." Before closing the door, he popped his head back in. "Chinese for dinner?" I nodded. "Let me know when you get hungry."

He closed the door behind himself and I lay down on the floor again, staring up at the ceiling fan. I tried to watch any one of the spokes as it went around in circles, but I kept losing my focus each time.

∽

I ran into Eva the next day walking into school.

"Hey, what's up with you? Are you okay?" She looked at me like we were friends. Like we were kids again.

"Huh?" Eva and I hadn't talked in years, not since my mom died, and I wasn't sure what would make her…Dee. Of course. Dee had decided to make friends for me. "Oh, uh, nothing. I'm fine. Umm, what's up with you?"

"Well, I'm confused about what's going on with you. You seemed fine when I talked to you a few weeks ago. Then you sit and have lunch with us and say you're coming to last weekend's party—which you didn't—because after begging to be my friend again, you disappeared for a week, didn't answer your phone, and now show up here as though there's nothing going on." The expectant look on her face was hard to take. I didn't owe her anything.

"That's quite the two weeks I've had," I said quietly under my breath, putting my hand up to my head to pull my hat off.

"What?"

"Nothing."

"Well?" she said. "So what's been going on?" There was that expectation again. I couldn't handle owing this much to this many people.

"It's just been a tough couple of weeks," I said, and she stared at me for a moment. What was I supposed to say? What did she want from me? Even if she and Dee had become best friends the week before, I wasn't just going to open up my whole life to her in the entrance to our school while we were being jostled by other kids coming in. If I would ever share with someone that I had been locked up in a mental institution, it wasn't going to be in this huge public space.

"And?" she asked, raising her eyebrows and using a gloved hand to push back her bangs.

"Nothing's been going on. Let's just pretend the last two weeks never happened, okay? We'll just go back to the way things were before." I wished I could do that with my whole life, well, except maybe that one day…that incredible feeling that I had that day. But, no, I needed to let Jamie go too.

"What? You are possibly the weirdest person I've ever met. I'm tired of this. You want to be friends. You don't want to be friends. You want to talk. You don't want to talk. I'm not going to try to keep up with you anymore. Screw this," and she walked into the building.

It was like a flashback to what had happened when my mom died. I remembered the day perfectly. I had just locked the stall in the bathroom when I'd heard the door open again. Eva and I had been friends for a long time, but I had noticed she'd been pulling away from me, so when I leaned down and recognized her shoes, I stayed as quiet as I could.

"I know she's going through a lot, but," she sighed heavily, "it's just been really hard on me. It's gotten to be too much. I don't know what else I can do for her. I don't know what she wants from me."

Whoever was with her hadn't said anything beyond a noncommittal "mmm." Eva responded by saying, "She's just gotten really difficult to deal with," before they left. Dee knew nothing about this kind of thing; she had never dealt with what I had dealt with.

I didn't need Eva. Or Dee. I was fine on my own.

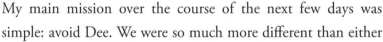

My main mission over the course of the next few days was simple: avoid Dee. We were so much more different than either of us had realized. I was tired of having to explain myself to her, tired of her judging me and thinking she was so much better than me. I was tired of all of it, tired of Dee. I didn't hate her, not really. I was just…exhausted from dealing with her.

She eventually caught up with me, though, on Sunday night. I'd sneaked a peek in the mirror to make sure I still looked the same as I remembered, and lo and behold, there was Dee waiting for me.

"Samara! Finally! I've been trying to catch you for like two weeks."

"Yeah, well, I wasn't allowed to have a mirror in rehab." *And I've been avoiding you*, I thought to myself.

"So what was it like? How was it? How do you feel?"

This was exactly what I was tired of with Dee. This sort of requirement to describe everything, to keep her up to date on everything all the time.

"Oh, wonderful. I'm all cured. Thanks, Dee. You obviously know what's best for me. I can't believe I ever doubted you."

"Samara, don't be like that," she said, just barely catching herself before she rolled her eyes at me.

We talked a little while longer, but eventually I couldn't stand her attitude so I just shook my head at her and walked away from the mirror. I don't know why I had expected Dee to understand; she had never acted like a friend. She had lied to me to get to know me and then sent me away just as I'd started trusting her.

As I closed the closet, my dad came in and stood silently for a moment. Then with one quick motion he looked under my bed and in my closet.

"Dad?"

"Who is in here with you? I keep thinking I hear someone talking to you or something. Before you left, it just happened late at night, but I thought I heard it again just now." He paused. "Your mother used to do the same thing."

"There's obviously nobody here."

He squinted and then walked out of the room muttering, but before pulling the door closed, he turned back to look at me. "Just a reminder: you have your support group tomorrow."

I wanted to tell him I wouldn't go, that I was tired of being his crazy daughter sent away for someone else to deal with, but I remembered what Sasha had said. I knew that her advice was better than anybody else's, so I just nodded.

I went to the group the next day. I hated the cliché of it all. The chairs were set up in a circle, and there was water in the corner for tea and coffee, and cookies on the table. It was all girls, and they were sitting in small groups talking about medals they had gotten or would be getting for reaching thirty-, sixty-, and ninety-day milestones. There was a group leader who began the meeting, and then everyone went around and introduced themselves, giving their names and why they were there.

"Hi. I'm Samara. I used to cut myself, but I stopped."

The girl next to me winked as I sat down and then stood up herself and said, "Hi, my name is Tanya, and today is the two-month anniversary of the last time I harmed myself." Everybody clapped, and the group leader walked over to Tanya and handed her a sixty-day medal.

I stayed after the group to talk to Tanya and some of the other girls. They were basically split into two groups: the girls who were there because their parents made them go and the girls who were there because they were really trying to quit whatever they had started. The first group was basically all still doing whatever they had been sent there for, and the girls in the second group were all somewhere between starting and quitting and starting again. And between those two groups was Tanya.

I went once a week. I wasn't sure if the group was really helping or not. I didn't think so, but it was a good way for me to see Tanya and it kept my father at bay. Things were easiest for me when he was out of the house. I wasn't talking to Dee. We'd catch glimpses of each other, but I think we had both given up on the idea of seeing each other regularly.

At the end of the third meeting, I was helping to put the chairs away, which seemed kind of pointless since another group came in after we did. They were just going to need to take the chairs and arrange them in a circle again on the floor of the dance studio. Tanya put a chair down, and it made a huge clatter. We did the best we could not to make eye contact so that we wouldn't burst out laughing because that would have just been too awkward in that silent room.

When we walked out of the studio, both of us burst out laughing. Holding it in that long made it that much funnier, and after a minute, we were literally holding each other up. When I was finally able to breathe normally again, I said, "Do you want to come over for a while?"

"Love to. How far are you?"

"Not far," I said and we walked to my house. When we got there, I took out my keys to go inside, but Tanya shook her head.

"You have this amazing porch! Let's stay out here for a while."

"It's freezing out. Let's go inside. It's all snowy."

Tanya looked around. "Don't you think it's pretty? Let's just sit outside for a while and look at the snow. It's so…something. I don't know." She brushed the snow off the edge of the porch, and we sat down with our feet on the top steps.

Tanya actually contrasted with the snow. She had really dark skin and a long black coat with a bright blue hat, gloves, and scarf. I smiled when I looked at her because that day she was wearing orange leg warmers.

"Leg warmers?" I said. "Really?"

"They're making a comeback. I'm telling you."

We watched as more and more people walked by, packing down the snow, dirtying it, and beginning the melting process.

"You always seem so happy in meetings," I said.

"Yeah, well, most of the time I'm drunk," she joked.

"Seriously, though, come on. You always seem, I don't know, light. Or something like that. I feel like I'm more depressed since I stopped cutting myself. Just because I'm not letting it out the same way. What did you do? Before you stopped? It's not cutting. I can always tell when someone else cuts."

She drew a line between us in the snow. I could tell she was thinking about making a joke, and I hoped she wouldn't. She looked up but didn't look directly at me.

"I hit myself. With a hammer. Mostly on my legs. Sometimes my arms. But I got one of my fingers pretty bad." She pulled off her bright blue glove and showed me that the skin under her pinky nail was still bruised. "I finally had to admit it was a problem."

"So how do you do it now? How do you seem so happy all the time? Seriously."

"Seriously? It's just because of my clothes," she said. "I wear really bright colors all the time. That makes it look like I'm happy." She pointed to her leg warmers. "I'm actually in a good mood on the days I'm wearing black and navy."

∾

I tried it, and it basically worked, certainly tricking my dad on the days I wasn't feeling so good. At least when I was wearing bright clothes I didn't have to talk about it.

Two weeks later, Tanya and I went out for coffee. She suggested the place, and I knew it seemed familiar when we walked in. It took me a second to register that it was where Dee and I had gotten coffee the day I had found out she was my reflection—the first time we met.

"You seem...off," Tanya said as we sat down.

"I'm fine. I just came here once with a friend who I don't really talk to anymore. I was just thinking about her. Sorry. I'm back now."

"No worries," she said. "What's going on with her? You guys have a falling-out?"

"Well, I guess so. She was the one who told my dad about my cutting and stuff." I watched closely to see how Tanya would react to that.

"I'm sure she thought it was the right thing to do."

"I'm tired of that excuse."

"What do you mean?" she asked.

"If people don't know what the right thing to do is, why don't they just ask? It's not that hard. A real friend would've done that."

"Hasn't that ever happened to you?" she asked. "You're sure that you know something, then you turn out to be wrong? Happens to me all the time. And then everyone tells me, 'If you weren't sure, why didn't you ask?' but I was sure. I was just wrong. Like you get an answer wrong on a test because you misunderstood the question instead of because you thought the question was unclear."

I sighed. "I guess."

I thought about Dee all the way home that night, and I decided it was time to find her again. Time to talk to her. It took a few nights of waiting.

∾

I was sitting at my desk, watching the mirror out of the corner of my eye, as I had each night for the last three nights. Finally, after all that waiting, I saw Dee.

"Hey," I said, getting up and walking toward her.

"Hi," she said quietly, looking at me.

"It's been a while. How are you?"

"Been better," she said sinking down to sit on the floor.

"Oh yeah? I'm, umm, I'm sorry." I waited to see if Dee was going to elaborate, but she didn't say anything. "How's, uh, how's Jamie doing? You two together still?"

"Jamie is fine," she said. "We've been really happy together. I'm afraid that might change soon. Once we established exactly what had happened while you were here, I was able to fix it. Well, I was able to fix it with Jamie anyway." She smiled and got a faraway look in her eyes for a moment. "To be honest, I just really love being with him."

Now I was the one with nothing to say. I waited.

137

"Well?" she said.

"Well what?" I asked.

"Maybe you owe me an apology."

"Maybe you owe me some thanks. I'm the one responsible for you and Jamie getting together, remember? I made it happen."

"Yeah, thanks a lot, Samara. You're absolutely right," she said sarcastically.

"You used to be so cool when we met. You understood what was going on. When did you become so selfish?"

"Selfish? Seriously? *I'm* selfish? All I've done is try to help you! And all you've done is try to shut me out. Try to ruin my life, try to ruin my relationships. You're the one who walks away every time things get even a little tough. You want to ditch me the way you ditched all your childhood friends?"

"Help me? *Help me?* I don't need your help, Dee. You never understood that. A friend, yes, but I didn't need you to be in charge of my life." I could hear myself screaming at her. I knew I hadn't meant for the conversation to go like this, but I couldn't help myself. "I basically raised myself. I've been taking care of myself for years. I don't need you to show me how."

"You know what, fuck it. Fuck you. I do everything to help you, and you never thank me and you never repay me. You just fuck up my life even more. You just screw me over and don't even have the decency to tell me. So fuck it all, Samara," Dee said.

I could see her eyes tearing up, but she didn't let herself cry. There was a steely determination to her face that I had never seen there before.

I did the best I could to control myself, but I just couldn't, and when I opened my mouth, all the stored-up anger came pouring out.

"Oh, yeah! You try spending a week in cutting rehab. You try explaining to a group of people you don't even like why you weren't in school for a week and didn't call any of them. It's your turn to be labeled as 'crazy.' I'm always going to *have been* in a mental institution, and it's because of you. Like I could have possibly screwed up your life any more than you screwed up mine. What the hell could I have done that was worse than this? Come on, Dee. What did I do? How did I screw up your perfect fucking life?"

"You slept with Jamie. You don't have to admit it. I know it's true." Her voice was quieting but it was angrier than I'd ever heard it. "You fucked him, Samara. And now I'm pregnant. Are you happy?" She breathed in sharply and clenched her fists. "You got me pregnant."

chapter 12

The Easier Way Out

Dee

We had only known each other for about three months, but I had become really dependent on Samara already. I looked forward to our conversations all day, and when she disappeared from my life, I knew it wasn't just that I was worried about her. I missed her. A lot. Since Jamie was the only person who knew about her, our conversations constantly revolved around where she was, what she was doing, and why she wasn't talking to me.

We were sitting in my favorite pizza place, Hot Pizzzza. I think everyone has one of these places. Everyone has a bagel store, a café, a bakery, somewhere that was the first type of that place they ever went to and nowhere else is ever quite as good. Hot Pizzzza is two-and-a-half blocks from my house, and there's a huge tree that takes up almost the entire expanse of the window. When I was little, I used to climb it in summer and eat the ices my mom bought me.

The people there all know me, and I'm sure I owe them a huge amount of money for all of the free food over the years, but nobody will take anything extra from me. I looked back at Jamie. "I just don't know what to do for her."

"She's going through a lot, Dee." He put his hand on top of mine. "She's gotta let it out somewhere. I'm just…" He stroked my hand. "I'm sorry it has to be you that has to deal with it."

"It's not dealing with it," I said, pulling away and pushing my hair back. "I don't mind. I just wish I could do more for her."

"You've done so much for her," he said. I was embarrassed when I felt myself tearing up. Jamie switched to my side of the booth and put an arm around me. "Hey, it's okay. It's all going to be okay. What you're doing…" He pulled me into him and rested his chin on the top of my head. "You're doing the best you can for her."

"Maybe I'm not. Maybe there's something I haven't thought of. Something I should be doing but I'm not. Something that would make things better for both of us."

Jamie was quiet, but he handed me a napkin from the dispenser.

"I'm sorry," I said, pulling away to look at him. "I don't know why I'm like this. I thought I had it all under control."

"Nothing to be sorry for." He pulled me close to him again. "You're dealing with a lot right now. It's way more than I've ever had on my mind."

"Thanks, Jamie. Look, I'm not feeling 100 percent. I think I'm just going to head home."

"What's the matter? Are you okay? Come on, I'll walk you," he said.

∾

My mother came home early that night. I heard her come in and

I got up to greet her, but the waves of nausea passed over me again and I had to lie back down.

She called me and I told her I was in my room. "Hey, sweetheart. You feeling okay?" she asked, kneeling down next to me and putting her hand on my forehead.

"Just a little sick, I think."

"Go back to sleep. We'll do our movie night another night, okay?" She wrapped the blankets more tightly around me.

"No, it's not that bad. We can do the movie tonight. Half an hour, okay?"

"Okay, sweetie. Try to sleep now." She kissed my forehead. "I'll wake you up in half an hour."

But she didn't wake me up. She was already gone when I got up the next morning, but she had left water and saltines next to my bed with a note saying, "Feel better. I left the movies if you want to watch. I'll try to be home early. Love, Mom."

When I was still getting sick on and off three-and-a-half weeks later, my mom insisted we go to the doctor. I had gotten sick in school once without telling her, but the second time I threw up after dinner she insisted it was time to get checked out.

We sat in Exam Room 5 for half an hour before Dr. Mensin came in. My mom grumbled about why the nurses didn't have to wear uniforms here but they had to wear uniforms where *she* worked. We could hear people shuffling around outside the door, but my mom insisted we keep it closed anyway.

Dr. Mensin had been my doctor since I was a baby, and since he had put on weight a few years ago, he had reminded me of Alfred Hitchcock. My mom had laughed when I told her that. I still had to sit on the butcher paper with dinosaurs and the alphabet.

We watched Dr. Mensin shuffle in. Answered the regular questions, "What's bothering us today?" and so forth. Then Dr. Mensin did all of the regular tests and came back into the room looking slightly upset.

"Do you mind if I talk to Lorna alone?" he asked my mom.

"No. That's fine." She understood these things. "Is everything all right?"

Dr. Mensin nodded.

"Then I'll be right outside. Let me know when you're finished." She looked back from me to him for a moment with a knowing look (what did she know that I didn't?) and then left and closed the door behind her.

Dr. Mensin continued staring into the folder for a moment after my mom left. "Lorna," he said, finally looking directly at me, "when's the last time you had intercourse?"

"What? Never." Samara. Samara had had sex. What had she and Jamie done to me? I knew Jamie had had sex before, but I couldn't imagine him giving me something.

He scratched his head and said, "This is going to be easier if you're honest with me."

"It's complicated," I told him.

"You're right, Lorna. It is complicated." He paused and looked down again, then back up at me. He sighed, finally making eye contact. "You're pregnant. You're going to have a baby."

I looked at him for a moment and laughed. "No, I…I can't be. This is not funny. I don't think this is funny at all."

"No, Lorna. It isn't funny. Now I know everyone thinks 'this can't happen to me,' but—"

"It can't happen to me."

"Lorna, I have the results right here."

"No. You don't understand. I can't be—"

I hadn't gotten pregnant. It wasn't me; I hadn't had sex with Jamie. We had just gotten past kissing. I couldn't be pregnant. It wasn't me. I couldn't believe…I couldn't deal with…I looked up at Dr. Mensin again.

"I'm p-p-pregnant?"

"That's right." He paused but I wasn't sure what he wanted me to say. "Now you can tell your mother or I can. But it has to be soon either way. You need to start thinking about your options: if you're going to abort, I'd like it to be within the first trimester, and if you aren't, then you're going to need prenatal care. I'd think about adoption as an option if you want to go to term. But we'll discuss your options at length with your mother. I want you to remember while you think about this that a baby is a huge responsibility for a young girl."

"I'm not that young. I'm not a little kid anymore." Everyone, even my mom and Samara, always acted like I was some kid who couldn't make her own decisions.

"Being pregnant doesn't make you an adult. As you begin to think about this, you really need to think about your future. Do you want to go to college? Will a baby let you do that? Would you be able to support a baby? And then you have to ask yourself the questions from the other side. Would you be able to give up a child? Is that something you could handle? I'd like to discuss this with your mother. In fact I'd like to do that right now so I'd like to tell her, but I want your permission to do so."

"I'll tell her. Please don't tell her. Let me tell her," I said, desperate to have control over something, anything anymore. My entire body was numb with shock, and I kept looking down at my stomach and touching it. I guess part of me expected my stomach to grow over the course of the conversation.

He sighed heavily. "All right, Lorna, but you have to tell her soon. I'm giving you the name of a gynecologist I've worked with for years." He handed me a prescription paper. "You need to tell your mom before anything else, though. Soon. Very, very soon."

"Yes, Dr. Mensin. I understand."

"All right then. I expect to see you very soon."

"Thank you, Dr. Mensin," I said, getting down off the table and going out into the hall to get my mom. She gave me a strange glance but didn't ask me any questions as the two of us walked to the car. The drive home was silent as I tried to figure out how I was going to break the news to my mother, and she gave me time to think about whatever Dr. Mensin had said to me.

It took me a week to figure out what to do. I stopped going to the literary magazine meetings after school. I avoided Jamie and came straight home and curled up in my bed every afternoon trying to figure out what to do next.

I was staring at the wall when my mom came in five days later. "Hi, Lorna."

"What?" I asked looking up at her.

"I just said hi. Head out of the clouds, sweetheart. I saw your math test on the table." I'd forgotten I'd left it there. "You failed? You've never failed before! I know precalc is hard, but it was your idea and you know I expect you to follow through."

"My head's not in the clouds. I've just been distracted. Leave me alone."

"Lorna—"

"No, Mom, just leave me alone. I need to be alone." I saw her take a step back. I didn't talk to my mom that way ever. "I'm sorry. I just…" I slumped down. "I'm sorry."

My mom walked out of the room without saying anything.

It was so frustrating. I was ashamed but I didn't think I should be. What had happened wasn't my fault, but I was going to be the one carrying it around or aborting it or doing whatever it was I was going to have to do.

❧

I felt betrayed. I was so angry at Samara. But at the same time, she was probably the only person who would really have good advice for me. Plus, I figured she would be one of the easier people to tell. Jamie and my mom were much too difficult. We hadn't talked in weeks, but I figured that once Samara knew about this, she would help me.

I wanted it to be a calm, collected conversation. I wanted to act like an adult. But Samara hadn't made that easy. The first thing she asked me about was how Jamie was, and knowing what the two of them had done, that got me pretty upset. But I tried to contain myself. I needed her help. But then she told me that I owed her a thank-you for getting me together with Jamie, and I lost whatever calmness I'd had.

I walked away right after blurting out that I was pregnant. I was feeling too woozy and light-headed to deal with her anymore.

❧

The next morning, Samara was at the mirror waiting for me.

"Who else knows?" she asked.

"Nobody," I told her, "just my doctor. I haven't had the guts to tell Jamie or Mom yet. I don't know, I thought maybe you'd have some advice about how to tell them. But in retrospect, I think you've contributed enough."

"You have to tell them soon, Dee," she said, as if I didn't already know that. I don't know what I was thinking, making her the first person to know.

I paused. What was she doing faking maturity here? "It's all well and good for you to say that, but unless you're going to tell them for me, well, I think you've already done your part. Don't you?"

"That's, that's what I wanted to say…" she said quietly. "I'll tell them if you want me to. We can switch places again. If you want to. I'll tell them. You shouldn't have to. It's small, but I want to do something to help. I'm so sorry. I had no idea this was going to happen. Do you want to switch places? Do you want me to try to talk to them?"

"I do," I said without thinking.

And we switched places. The tingly feeling surprised me, even though I had felt it before. And the feeling of being in someone else's body. Even with Samara's offer to help, I was still unbelievably mad at her, and it was hard to pretend we were going to be all right.

Part of me knew even as we did it that this had been the wrong decision. I knew it would be better if I told them myself. Then at least I would know how they found out. What their reactions were, how they were going to treat me. It had to be handled delicately. But I didn't know how, and right then, having Samara tell them seemed easier. Dr. Mensin would tell my mother soon if I didn't. And all I could think was that I had enough challenges coming up in the months ahead and I knew it was going to be hard. The easier way out was all right with me. Just this one time. Just for this one thing.

chapter 13

Watching Over Me

Samara

I paced around my room in circles, trying to figure out what to do. Eventually, when my room started to feel too small, I began pacing around the house: the living room, the kitchen, the dining room, and my dad's empty bedroom, repeating the day that I had spent with Jamie in my head.

I didn't suggest the switch. I didn't force Jamie. It's my fault...of course, it's my fault. But I didn't mean for this to happen. I didn't mean for any of this to happen. What have I done? What is Dee going to do? Is she going to keep it? She can't keep it. What's she going to tell her mom and how?

Her mom will never understand this, that it wasn't the real Dee; she's not going to believe it. There's no way to make her mom understand. Why should Dee have to deal with this? I want to do something; I want to help. But there's nothing I can do. Well, maybe there is. At least I can take over the responsibility of telling Dee's mom and Jamie. It's hardly anything. But I guess it's something.

∼

As I looked around Dee's room, I did my best to accept that this might be the last time I saw it. Even when we were arguing, I still believed that Dee and I would make up, that we would be there for each other. But I had screwed up big time, and it would be over after this. After this, I was going to have to stay in my own world.

Even from inside Dee's room I could smell fresh waffles in the kitchen. I opened the door and walked into the kitchen.

"I heard you up and around, so I figured I'd make breakfast. What do you want on your waffles?"

"Umm, oh, umm, I don't know. Whatever you think." I watched her floating around the kitchen in her ratty blue bathrobe with yellow moons, her hair not done yet, wearing her glasses instead of contacts. "Can you, uh, can you sit down for a minute? I have to tell you something."

She turned around, and I guess she caught sight of my face and sat down at the table with me without saying anything.

As soon as she sat down, I popped up and started pacing. I couldn't look at her while I told her this.

"I'm not sure…I'm not sure how to tell you this."

"Just tell me, sweetheart. It's okay. Just tell me."

"I'm…" I stopped pacing and looked down at the floor, taking a deep breath. "I'm pregnant."

She pulled her glasses off and ran her hands over her face, rubbing her eyes for a moment and then looking back up at me. "I guess, uh, I guess I wish I was more surprised." I hadn't realized that Dee's mom knew about what had happened with me and Jamie, but I guess she saw more than I realized. "You weren't careful? Safe? I can't believe that. We've talked about this, Lorna. You should've known."

I had told myself that at least a dozen times over the course of the last night, asked myself the same questions. I had been on birth control for years, so it hadn't occurred to me to think about the fact that Dee wasn't. I knew that Jamie had been with other girls before, but he seemed to imply that he was clean. I should have asked explicitly. I always did when it was my body. Why was I so stupid with him? So careless with someone else's body? I couldn't believe I had let this happen to Dee. All I could think to say was, "I'm sorry. I didn't plan this."

"Jamie?" she asked suddenly, looking up at me.

"What? Yes. Yes, of course."

"Well, I don't know. I don't feel like I know you at all anymore." She stood up and walked over to the waffle iron, which was now smoking. She pulled the plug out and took the burnt waffle off the iron, stuffing it down the garbage disposal. "I don't know what to say, Lorna. What are we going to do?"

"I'm so sorry, Mom." I bit back tears as I watched her stomp around the kitchen. "But I really need you."

"You got yourself into this, Lorna. I don't know what you want from me." She turned back to the sink, turned on the water, and flipped on the disposal.

"Please listen to me," I yelled over the disposal. "You once told me everyone has more than one face."

She continued staring at the wall behind the sink, but she turned off the disposal. "I never told *you* that," she said quietly.

"This wasn't me that did this. It was my...my other face. My other self. My irresponsible self. The self that I usually contain entirely. But the responsible me, well, I'm trying to fix it."

I saw her tears falling into the sink, and I was so upset. I couldn't believe I had hurt her this way. I looked at her back. I couldn't believe I had done this to her, to her daughter.

"Please don't turn on me, Mom. I need you now more than ever. Please don't turn your back on me." I felt myself get quieter and whispered to myself, "You don't know what it's like to not have a mother."

She turned around and stared at me, furrowing her eyebrows and squinting to see me properly. She ran her hands over her face again and shook her head back and forth. "Neither do you, Lorna?" I almost smiled in spite of myself: she had allowed her voice to go up at the end of her sentence, something she had specifically warned me about the last time I was there.

"And I don't want to."

She shook her head, but I could see that I had struck home. She walked over and put her arms around me, but I could feel her body still shaking from the news.

"How did this happen? What do you see in him?"

I wasn't sure how to answer that question, so I just pulled up all the things I had been forcing myself to pretend I wasn't thinking. "He's…he's a great guy. He's sweet and caring. And he worries about making me happy and comfortable and…and he loves me, Mom."

She sighed. "You're sixteen. You really think you can recognize if he loves you or not? He's your first boyfriend. Don't get ahead of yourself."

"He's not my—" I cut myself off. *He's not mine at all.* I sat there silently for a few minutes. This had been harder than I expected it to be. "If I'm not, umm, if I'm not keeping it, do I still need to tell Jamie?"

"What? Yes, of course. Of course you have to tell him. He doesn't know? You haven't talked to him yet? How long have *you* known?"

"I don't know, a week?" I had no idea how long Dee had known. "But Jamie doesn't know yet. I wanted to…I want to tell him today. I need to get it over with."

"You want to get the talking to the boy you say you're in love with over with. Okay. Fine. Go. Find him, come back here, and we'll talk. Good, I need some time to think. Tell him that I want to speak to his parents. You two can't deal with this alone." I looked at her for a moment but didn't move. "Go."

Without saying anything, I turned and took Dee's coat and walked out the door.

∽

I started walking toward the school, realizing that I didn't know where Jamie lived. I remembered the park he had taken me to the first day Dee and I had switched, and when I reached the school, I changed directions and tried to retrace my steps and find the park. There he was, pacing in circles and looking like he was waiting for someone.

I walked toward him. "Jamie!"

"Dee? What's going on? I haven't talked to you in…over a week. You've been avoiding me. Are you okay? Is everything okay? What are you doing in the park in this weather?" I smiled at the thought of Jamie worrying that snow on the ground would somehow hurt Dee.

"Looking for you. And I'm not Dee."

"Samara? Oh no. Not this shit again," he said, shaking his head and backing away.

"I swear this will be the last time. Dee asked me to talk to you about something. The time…the time you had sex. Well, it wasn't, umm, it wasn't with Dee. It was with me."

Jamie stared at me for a moment and then pursed his lips and nodded. "I know."

"What, you knew? You knew the whole time?" I tried to suppress the little jump in the pit of my stomach.

"I don't know. Maybe. I guess I suspected that day but I was excited. You guys switched back that night though, right? I knew when I saw Dee that night that it wasn't her. Or that it hadn't been her earlier. You know what? This is too complicated. If you're done switching places, if that's all you had to tell me, just go. I don't know what's going on with Dee, and I don't want to talk to you about it. I want to talk to her."

"It was Dee who asked me to come talk to you. That's not all I had to tell you."

"What more is there?"

I stared at him, trying to figure out how to say it. Trying to figure out what to do. I didn't want to be responsible for dropping this bomb. "I…I mean, Dee, well, Dee is pregnant."

Jamie quickly developed a green tinge and spluttered, "You mean, I…we…pregnant?"

We. Hearing him say that made it more real. *We* got Dee pregnant. She had nothing to do with it. *We* got Dee pregnant. I nodded at Jamie.

"I don't understand. How could this happen? It was just one time. We were just…we were just fooling around. It was just one time. When you didn't…I just assumed you were on birth control or something." We stared at each other, each silently blaming the other for winding up in this mess. For doing this.

"Well, I guess one time really is enough. Listen, here's the thing. I don't know what Dee is going to do, but whatever it is, you need to support her. Let her make the decisions, not you." Jamie nodded numbly.

"Oh, and her mom wants to talk to your parents." I was sure he hadn't heard anything I had said after the word "pregnant." "This is going to be the last time we see each other." He just stared at me. "Good-bye, Jamie."

I turned and walked away, leaving him standing in the park, all the color drained from his face and replaced by a light green.

When I got back to Dee's apartment, her mom was asleep. I pulled a blanket over her and wanted desperately to wipe the tears from her face, but I knew it would be better if Dee woke her. I went back into Dee's room and looked in the mirror, where Dee was waiting.

❧

The first thing I did when I got home was to sit down at my desk and put my head in my hands. *God,* I thought, *I wish I had a mother like that. Or anyone who cares the way she cares. I know*

Tanya cares, but a friend just isn't the same thing as a mother. And I need a mother. Or a father. But my father is never going to pay attention. I need someone. Something. And without thinking, I grabbed a blank piece of stationery.

Dear Mom,

Today I fessed up to a mistake I made. It's hard to explain, but I got a really good friend into a lot of trouble. I wish you had been here to tell me it was the wrong thing to do. It's almost five years later, and I still don't understand how you could leave me to face my teenage years alone. You should have been here to tell me all of the things Dad never told me about being a teenager. He was too afraid all the time, and I wish you had been…I think you should have been here to guide me.

You left me alone, Mom. I'm trying to fix things, but I don't know how. Two nights ago, I sat in my closet for three hours waiting for you to come tell me everything was going to be all right and tempt me out with cookies and a movie. But you weren't coming, were you? Neither was Dad. I know he still loves me, still loves you, but sometimes I wonder if he would notice if I just disappeared altogether. Would you notice? If there is a heaven, and I doubt there is, would you look for me if I got there? Or would it just be another place where I'm all alone all the time?

I need someone to explain what's going on with Dee's baby. Is it mine? I'm not ready to be a mother. God, I still write letters to my own dead mother. What happened? You know what, Mom? If the baby is mine, if Dee asks me to take care of it, I'll never leave it. Not like you. I can be stronger. I would never do to a little baby what you did to me. I'm angry, Mom. I'm tired of being sad. I'm angry. You didn't even think of me when you did this. And I'm mad at you for that. But I need your help. I don't know what to feel. What do I do?

Love,

Samara

I stuffed the letter into a matching butterfly envelope and addressed it, "Mom." I left the letter on my desk and stared at it for a long time. It was years since I had written to my mother. Part of me missed that. Part of me was embarrassed. I knew she would never read these letters anyway. I opened my dresser and pulled out a lighter, flicked it on and off, and picked up the letter. I stared at the flame and the letter, eventually letting go of the letter and letting it drop back onto my desk. I couldn't bring myself to do it.

Mom, please take this letter. Read it. Help me figure out what to do. I left the letter on my desk and found a small hand mirror in the closet. I stood it up on my nightstand so that Dee could wake me up if she needed to and then climbed into bed. I tossed and turned for a little while but eventually fell into a deep sleep. I slept better that night than I had in weeks.

When I woke up the next morning, the letter was gone from my desk. I didn't know what had happened. I remembered flicking the lighter on and off, but I was sure I had left it on my desk in the end. I hadn't burned it. There weren't ashes anywhere. I stared at the empty space and looked under my desk, under the piles of stuff, on the floor, and began to wonder...*Did my mom take it? Maybe there really is a heaven; maybe she really is watching over me. No,* I told myself firmly, *no, it just fell or something. I burned it but I forgot. Mom is gone.*

chapter 14

So Desperately Wanted

Dee

I looked around Samara's room, waiting. I had nothing to do. I walked in circles, feeling very small. It was hardly a comfort to know I wouldn't be responsible for telling my mom. I wasn't sure if Samara was planning on finding Jamie after she talked to my mom; I hoped so.

I didn't know how I would tell him if I had to. It used to be so easy to talk to Jamie, but it seemed like years ago that I had sat in my bedroom watching him toss a ball up and down and discussing with him how to get Samara to talk to me. It could have been decades since Jamie first suggested the mirror as the location of the alternate universe.

I sat down with my legs crossed in the middle of the room. I didn't belong here. I was stuck in this world where nobody else I knew belonged, where *I* didn't belong. I found myself back in front of the closet door, back in front of the mirror. I looked into the eyes of Samara's reflection for a moment. I remembered when I became curious about my reflection, about the other world, and for the first time I wondered why Jamie had never tried to get through the mirror or even asked about his reflection.

I wanted Jamie to be more curious than he was. I desperately wanted him to question what was happening in Samara's world, what was happening between me and her. But for some reason, since I'd gotten back he hadn't asked me a single question about Samara. Sometimes, he'd let me bring her up, but he never asked anything specific.

I realized then that this would be my last time in her world. I looked down at Samara's arms and legs, trying to memorize everything about her, and smiled in relief when I saw that the scars were healing and there were no new ones to take their places. I stood up slowly and stepped out of Samara's room, closing the door behind me.

I looked around the house. It was just the sort my mom had always wanted. Spacious but homey. It looked lived in, which was funny because I knew neither Samara nor her dad spent much time there. If my mom had this house, she would spend all her time here. Samara's mom seemed to have spent a lot of time here when she was alive, and I wondered if the life of the house still came from her. I wondered if my mom and Samara's mom had ever known each other or thought about each other. If her mom had known she had my mom's dream house.

"Dad?" I called. But of course he wasn't home. I went back into Samara's room to sit and wait in front of the mirror, unsure of how long this would all take. Just as I walked in, a snowball hit her window. I looked desperately around the room, trying to figure out who the girl at the bottom of the window was. I found a picture with the caption, *Tanya and Me*, in a frame on the shelf above her desk. I opened the window and stuck my head out. Tanya was one of the prettiest girls I had ever seen. She was wearing a black coat and a bright blue hat, scarf, and gloves.

"Come out and play with me," she said.

"Later. I can't right now."

"No, now. I'm lonely. Come play with me."

"I'm not dressed yet. Sorry." It seemed like a reasonable excuse.

"I've got time. Come outside and have a snowball fight."

"Come back tomorrow. I'm sick. I don't feel well today."

"That isn't true," she yelled up, and even from far away I could see she looked hurt. I had tried making Samara friends, and I was told that all I had done was screw things up. I wasn't getting involved again.

"All right, it's not true. But I can't come out right now. I don't want to have a snowball fight. Can you please leave me alone?" I asked. Why should I have to deal with this, given the amount I was going to have to deal with when I got home?

"I thought we had plans. I thought we were going to get dinner and see a movie. If we have a snowball fight now, we'll have time to change before the movie."

Change into what? I wondered. She didn't have a bag with her. "I just don't want to go out today, okay?"

"Yeah, sure," she said. "I'll just…leave you to your thoughts."

I watched as the footprints she'd left while she walked away were covered again by snow swirling in the wind. It took a few minutes, but I realized all of the sudden how cold I was standing by the window and I closed it, shivering. Then I went back over to Samara's closet and sat down to wait. I couldn't imagine what was taking so long.

"Mom, I'm pregnant." That was all she had to say, and then she'd come back. I would've done it; I just couldn't bear to see the look of angry disappointment that I knew was coming.

I was angry. I was angry at everyone and at no one. I was angry at the whole world for getting me into this mess. It wasn't just Samara or Jamie; I was just angry. The only thing I can remember thinking about as I sat waiting for Samara to come back was my anger and what anger must look like when it pulses through you. I looked at my arms and wondered where the anger was, where it stopped and where it started.

I hated anger, but I didn't know what else to feel so I let it consume me as I waited and waited and waited. I watched my eyes, *Samara's eyes*, in the mirror, wondering where the anger was in my head at that moment.

When she finally came back, the anger was unbearable. "Took you long enough," I snapped.

"Sorry," she said looking down. "I told your mom. And Jamie. Your mom said she wasn't surprised. Why wasn't she surprised?"

"That afternoon, Jamie snuck out the window, right?"

"Yeah…" she said.

"Well, she heard him. She told me so. It's the only way I figured out I was supposed to have had sex with Jamie."

"Oh." Samara paused for a moment. "I just…I'm so sorry, Dee.

"Yeah, well, you should be."

"I just…there's something I want to say." I looked at her and waited for her to continue. "If you decide to, umm, to have it taken care of…if you decide to get an abortion, I'll switch back with you again. I mean, I'll do it. You shouldn't have to. I wish there was more I could do for you."

I stared at her. I hadn't even really thought about that. I wasn't sure what I wanted to do. "What did Jamie say? It's not just mine or yours, or whatever. It's his too."

"He said he'd support whatever decision you make."

"That doesn't sound like him. He usually has his own opinions. It's one of the things I love about him," I said.

She shrugged and shook her head. "Talk to him about it, I guess. I don't know. He was kind of in shock after I told him, but he seemed like he'd do whatever you want. Oh, and your mom, she wants to meet Jamie's parents and talk to them about it."

"What? Why? Did you say that was okay?"

"I didn't…" Her eyes got big. "I didn't realize that was bad. I mean, remember, we need adults involved? Remember telling my dad? If you think being pregnant is entirely just…it's no smaller than my cutting was."

"There *was* someone who knows better involved. My mom."

"She was the one who said she wanted to talk to them. I didn't suggest it, Dee. Why are you freaking out?"

Why was I freaking out? Because I didn't know what Jamie was thinking? Because I didn't know what his parents would say about me? Would think about me? Because I hardly knew who I was anymore and felt unable to make a good impression on someone else?

"All you were supposed to do was tell my mom. You weren't supposed to make other plans for me."

"Well, I'm sorry," she said quietly.

We sat silently and stared at each other. Finally I broke the silence. "Let's just switch back."

"Fine," she said. And we stepped into the mirror at the same time and switched back. When we turned around to look at each other, I realized that this might be the last time we would see each other.

"Samara, wait."

She looked at me, and I could see that her eyes were watery. It took a moment for me to put my hand up to my face and realize that my face was tear-streaked too. What did I want to say? What could I say? The anger had dissipated. Now it was just me and her. Standing and staring at each other.

"Thank you. For everything. Everything is all messed up," I said. "This isn't what I wanted when I started looking for you. I don't think…I don't know if we're going to see each other again."

She nodded. "You gave me so much, Dee. I'm sorry for everything."

At a loss for words, I simply raised my right hand and waved to her. At the exact same moment, Samara raised her left hand and waved back. And with watery smiles to each other, we turned and walked away from our mirrors.

෴

I walked out into the living room and saw my mom was asleep. I thought about waking her up, but I decided that it would be easier if she woke up without me and had some time to decompress. I went back into my room and left the door a tiny bit open, waiting for my mom to come in. Wondering what I would say to her when she did.

Finally I heard a tentative knock on the door. My mom came in without waiting for a response.

"Come into the kitchen, please. Dr. Bentley has a few abortion doctors he recommends. I'll ask him, and we'll talk to Dr. Mensin and try to get this done as soon as possible."

"Abortion?"

"What else are you planning to do? You're not in a position to raise a baby. You have no income. The father is an irresponsible—"

"He is not! He's a great guy!" I felt my anger flare up again. Why was I feeling this way?

"He's a child. You're a child. What are you thinking? You used to be so logical. What happened, Lorna?"

"I can do this. And Jamie will help. I know him. I know he will. What right do you have to say I can't? To decide for me that I *have* to have an abortion? Maybe I want to keep the baby."

I wasn't sure why I was so angry. Not having the baby really did seem like the best thing to do. But everyone always thought of me as being so young and so incapable. It just didn't seem fair that my mother had decided this without me. It wasn't a question; it was an order. I watched her eyes roll back in her head, and she stared around the kitchen before finally looking back at me.

"Have you thought about this at all?" she asked me. "Have you thought about it even a little? How are you planning on taking care of a baby? You are apparently not even capable of taking care of yourself."

"What?"

"You're pregnant, Lorna."

"I didn't do this *to* you, Mom. Of course, I've thought about it." Actually, I hadn't thought about it. "I'll get a job, and Jamie will get a job. And we can…we can work it out."

"Does Jamie even know about this grand plan of yours? Does he know you want to have a baby with him? Does he know what that means?"

"We might not have worked out all the details yet…" I trailed off at the end.

She crossed her arms and leaned back and closed her eyes. "Sweetheart, let's stop and think about this. Let's both try to calm down. What did Jamie say when you told him?"

"He was, umm…" Samara hadn't told me. "He was surprised. I'm giving him some time to digest. It's his baby too, you know."

"I do know. I think I understand that slightly better than you."

"No, Mom, you don't." I felt my hand jump to my stomach, feeling for the thing we, the thing Samara and Jamie, had created out of nothingness.

"Did you remember to tell him I want to talk to his parents? They should be involved in this. It's their…grandchild too. Wow. Grandchild. You're making me a grandmother."

"I'll make sure he understands that." I paused and she watched me. "I'm tired, Mom. Can I go lie down?"

"Fine. Go. But if you think you're tired now, just wait until you have a baby."

I walked out of the kitchen without looking back at her.

I lay in bed wondering what I was going to do. Why had I gotten so angry with my mom? She was right, wasn't she? She was always right…but I put my arms around my stomach. I wanted this baby. My baby. Jamie's baby. I thought about how much my mom loved me, and I wanted something to love that way. She was mad at me, and she still loved me. I knew that a baby wasn't a good way to keep a couple together—my parents were proof of that—but I still wondered. I put that idea out of my head.

I wanted to talk to Samara. What had she told him? What had she told my mom? A part of me wanted her advice too. What should I do? I walked over to my closet mirror and saw that Samara was still there. She was sleeping, but I could still get in. I stepped from my bedroom into Samara's and looked at her. She looked so peaceful. I wondered how she could be so peaceful when so much was going on. I took a step back. I didn't want to wake her up because she was done with me. I could tell.

I looked around her room for the last time, and something caught my eye. There was a letter on her desk. I walked over to look at it. "Mom," it read on the front. I don't know why, but I picked it up and looked at it. I put it in my pocket before walking over to Samara's bed, kissing her forehead, and disappearing back into my own room.

"Dear Mom…" Even knowing how much worse my own situation was, when I finished reading the letter, I still wanted to take Samara in my arms and hold her and rock her and tell her everything would be okay. Just the same way my mother used to do when I had nightmares. But this wasn't Samara's nightmare; this was Samara's life.

My life…it was my life that was ruined. I wished I could bring her mother back, but I couldn't. Between the two moms, they could have figured everything out. What had happened to us? What was happening to our lives? How had we gotten here?

How had everything gotten so out of hand? I'd thought I had a plan. I'd just wanted a friend to talk to. And now…*I'm a pregnant teenager. And Samara just got out of rehab.*

I wondered, only for a moment, if I was Samara's angel. And my mother was her mother as an angel. I wanted it to be true because I wanted to tell Samara that her mother still cared about her, that she was still watching. But I didn't want to tell her that I had read her personal letter to her mom. I don't even know what made me do it. I didn't go through other people's personal things. That wasn't me.

As I read and reread the letter, getting choked up by the end every time, I realized that the real problem was that Samara had never had the chance to say good-bye to her mother. That was what she really needed to do. And that was what she so desperately wanted to do.

chapter 15

Broken Down

Samara

Before long, Tanya and I were spending weekends together. She would come over on Friday afternoons, and we'd watch movies. Tanya was a huge Audrey Hepburn fan, so we watched a lot of the classics.

Tanya was finishing up senior year, so she didn't have much to do besides show up to school once in a while. I probably should have been working harder. My teachers kept reminding us that junior year is extremely important for getting into college. But since this had all started, I just hadn't been able to focus on my schoolwork.

One weekend, Tanya went into the guest room and announced, "It's boring in here."

"What?"

"Well, I've been sleeping in this room two or three nights a week for the last three weeks, and I think it's boring in here. It needs decoration. Doesn't look like me at all."

"Maybe that's because it's not yours!" I said, laughing. "This is my dad's house. We can't just redecorate his guest room."

She raised her eyebrows at me. "Would he even notice? I mean, does your dad even live here anymore? I've met him twice now, and I've slept here, again, how many nights?"

I sighed. "He says he travels so he can save for me to go to a good college. Not like your parents are much better. Do they even know you're not coming home this weekend?"

"My dad does. He'll tell my mom," she said, pausing for a moment to walk over to the wall and run her hands along it. "We could repaint."

"No, we can't." I laughed again.

"Fine. Then let's do your room.'"

I shook my head. "I like my room. Although…"

"Although?" she perked up.

"I was thinking about…" How could I phrase this without arousing suspicion? "Changing the closet around a little bit."

"The closet? That's all you'll give me?" she asked. "You can just close the door on everything I do."

"Well, we can cover the whole door, inside and out. You know, over the mirror and the whole rest of the door."

"Cover up your mirror? But you're so pretty." She stuck her lower lip out. "You don't want to see yourself anymore?"

"I would rather see your fancy decorations."

"Okay. I'll do it," she said.

"Awesome. Okay. Bedtime. But let's do my room tomorrow."

"Fine. Good night," she said, pulling her pajamas out of the top drawer. "My toothbrush is the…"

"Orange one," I said, knowing that she already knew.

I woke up the next morning and went out to buy muffins. When I walked back in, Tanya was making coffee. "Honey, I'm hooome," I called.

She turned around. "Massive headache. What were we drinking last night?"

"I was drinking Coke. What were you drinking?" I said, watching her sip at her coffee.

"Whatever was in the flask I swiped from my dad," she said.

I took the muffins out of the bag and grabbed a plate from the cabinet, pushing the pizza box from the night before behind the trash can. "So, have you thought about what we can do with the closet door in my room?" I asked, attempting nonchalance.

"Yes, I have!" she said. "I think we should do a collage of posters. Audrey Hepburn, of course, and then Marilyn Monroe. Did you know she was like a size 12 or something? Come on," she said, grabbing the coffeepot and the plate of muffins, "let's go eat outside."

I guess Tanya had enough quirks that my wanting to cover up my mirror didn't really bother her. I pulled my coat on and followed her out onto the porch. It was still cold, even if it was warm for February.

We spent most of that Saturday wandering around trying to find enough posters to cover up my mirror. When we had enough, Tanya taped them all together and then taped them above the mirror as a sort of curtain on that side. She painted a small mural on the other side, a neighborhood of cookie-cutter houses all in a row. Like Dee's neighborhood. But not like her house. Not like Dee herself.

∾

By the time my dad got back from his trip, I had covered all of the mirrors in the house except the one in his bedroom. For some reason, I guess I didn't think my dad would notice. He didn't notice much else lately. I was rinsing makeup off when he walked past the bathroom Monday night and popped his head in.

"Samara, what's going on here?" he asked, tugging at the light blue curtain I had put over the bathroom mirror.

"Hmm? Oh. I covered the mirrors," I said, trying to sound light and cheerful and to walk away before he figured out how to respond.

"Why?" It was a logical question. But I couldn't come up with an answer fast enough.

"It doesn't matter to you. You're never here anyway. I left the one in your room. You can look in the mirror there."

"Well, I appreciate that, but why are the rest of the mirrors covered?"

"My support group," I blurted out before I was sure where the explanation was going. "They told me to focus on my inner self by not seeing my outer self." My support group—Tanya—had helped me. And that *was* what they'd said in rehab. So it was kind of true.

His hand dropped and he said, "Oh. I guess that's a good idea then."

∽

I tried to focus on my schoolwork. A new semester was starting and I settled back into the mundane pretty well, but I had trouble keeping Dee and Jamie out of my mind. A few weekends later, I tried to explain my situation to Tanya without really telling her anything.

We were sitting in my living room, and she was painting my toenails bright green. She says that one of the awesome things about winter is that since you always have to wear shoes, you can paint your toenails any color you want. I almost hadn't let her. I was actually that embarrassed by how long it was since I'd shaved my legs. But it was winter, and, well, I had run out of razors a long time ago.

I had taken down the mirror hanging over the fireplace instead of covering it since that one seemed too conspicuous to cover. It was behind the piano facing backward. I looked over and saw it and felt a small shudder between my shoulders.

"There's something I wanted to tell you. I've been having kind of a hard time lately," I began.

"I've noticed," Tanya replied. "And lately? It's been what, three or four months now? And you've looked horrible since we covered your mirror. I mean, come on, have you even seen yourself? I've been waiting for you to bring it up because I felt bad, but what happened in the last few months?"

Four months, I thought. Four months since I had seen Dee. Since I had seen Jamie. Heard about the baby that they would be having together. Without me. But instead of saying all that, I said, "Yeah. See, I have this friend, and I got her into some trouble."

"What kind of trouble?"

"It doesn't matter."

"It does matter."

"Some trouble with a guy and her mother. Life trouble. Then I tried to fix it, but she seems like she doesn't even want my help

173

anymore. I haven't seen her in months. And I can't talk to her now because she wouldn't listen even if I tried."

"So you just gave up on her? You just gave up on your friend? Were you two close?" she asked.

"Yeah, we were, but I don't know, things just went downhill."

"If things got tough with us, would you just give up on me?"

"No, of course not. It's totally different with you and me." I looked down at my toenails. "Wanna do the same color on my hands?"

"Really?" she said, and I nodded. "Yeah, give me your hand." I did. "Look, if my friends had just given up on me, where would I be now?"

"What do you mean?" I asked her.

"Well, they're the ones who turned me in. I know I told you that it was after I crushed my finger, and it was, sort of. I started wearing gloves all the time, but I took them off one day and a couple of my friends saw my finger and took me to the hospital. They talked to our school shrink. They made me go to our support group. That's how we met."

I looked down at her hands. She couldn't paint her nails because of the bruise, but I could see it was almost healed. She saw me staring and pulled her hand back. They *had* done the right thing.

"Can I take a guess at something?" she asked.

"Shoot."

"Was this the friend that got you into our support group?"

"Well," I thought for a second, "she's the one who turned me in to my dad. So I guess so. She's the one who sent me to rehab."

"Forgive her."

I looked over at the mirror that was turned around behind the piano. "She won't talk to me," I said.

"Forgive her. She's responsible for us meeting. If our friends hadn't been watching out for us, we never would have met."

"Fate?"

"Maybe," she said, shrugging. "Other hand." I gave her my other hand.

"But what if I think fate is telling me I shouldn't talk to her again? What if fate says to give up? What then? What if my decision is to give up a friend?"

"Then you wouldn't have had to ask me."

Tanya didn't know the whole story, though, and I wondered what she would've said if she did know the truth.

∾

When Dad was home the next weekend, he suggested we go shopping. Being gone so much, he said he was worried about what I was eating all the time. And I was running out of shampoo too, so I agreed.

We had some trouble making conversation in the car. He told me more about the new—well, not so new anymore—job. It sounded like he was happy. It was a good fit for him. I told him I was taking an art class for my elective.

"I design in it."

"Like when you were little? With your mom?" he asked, looking at me out of the corner of his eye.

I nodded. "I think I'm okay at it. I'm going to try actually making a dress at some point. Right now, it's just drawings."

We pulled into the grocery-store parking lot. As we pushed the cart around the store, grabbing as much freezer food as possible, it started to feel more natural being together. Until we got to the aisle with home goods. I put the shampoo in the cart fine. But when I picked up razors, my dad shook his head. He took them and put them back on the shelf.

"Sam, do you really think that's a good idea?" I noticed he was looking down at my arms. I picked them up and reached them out to him.

"Nothing," I said. "I told you I stopped."

"Then, what's going on with the mirrors still? What happened to the one in the living room?" I had thrown it away after my talk with Tanya because I didn't want to be tempted. I just couldn't see Dee yet. "Do you really think you can handle having razors back again?"

"Dad, if I wanted to be cutting myself, I would. And if it makes me more comfortable, does it really matter what I did with the mirrors? Or why?"

"I'm trying to be supportive, Sam. I'm doing the best I can. I'm trying to understand."

"Then understand that I want to shave my legs." I said it louder than I intended, but he still looked skeptical. "Look," I said, hearing my voice rise, "you're gone all the time. You leave money under the plates. Great. Thanks. If I wanted to buy razors to break and cut myself with, I would."

I was crying. In the grocery store. "I just want to be normal," I said, leaning back on one of the shelves and covering my face with my hands. "I want you to stop treating me like I'm some crazy kid. I want to shave my legs like a regular teenager. I want you to stop looking at my arms instead of at my face. This is why I didn't want to go to rehab. I knew it would be like this. I knew. I knew you would always see me like this, and I just want to be normal."

"Okay. Okay, Sam. I'm sorry. Come here," he said, and put his arms around me. Over his shoulder, I saw Eva backing out of the aisle, eyes wide. *Great, another thing she can think I'm a freak for.*

Everything wasn't fixed. He was still hardly around; he couldn't help it. He couldn't quit his job. But at least he let me buy razors and shave my legs. At least he looked at my face when we got home.

It was a sunny, beautiful day. The trees on my block were all budding, and it was just warm enough that a T-shirt without a jacket was fine. Tanya was sitting on my porch in a neon green shirt and a long brown skirt with big blue stripes. I was on my way home from school, and I was thinking about how there were only three more days until I was done with this year. Until summer, when I could do whatever I wanted and not have to worry. Tanya jumped up when she saw me.

"Guess what!"

"What?" I asked.

"I'm leaving. I'm going away."

"For how long? Where?"

"Forever. And Tucson, Arizona."

"Why Tucson?"

"I've read all about it," she said, pacing up and down the stairs. "I'll get a job raising chickens. It's hot and dry, so it won't snow all winter. It's not here. The people who know me here aren't there, and the people there don't know me. I can be anyone. I can do whatever I want."

"But you can't leave. I need you. You can be anyone you want here. You said never give up on a friend. I don't want you to leave." I couldn't believe what she was saying. I felt myself getting worked up, getting scared.

"Why do you think I'm here? Come with me. We'll raise chickens, and one day we'll start our own farm. Imagine it. Leave all this behind. Forget rehab. Forget homework and parents who don't listen to anything we say, who aren't even around. Forget winter and muggy, horrible weather. Forget the support group. I just go to see you anyway.

"Forget it all. Come with me. We have the money between us. I'm eighteen so I'll sign whatever needs to be signed. We'll both close out our bank accounts and we'll go. Let's do it. Come on."

"We can't just up and leave. What about our lives?" I asked, but I could already feel a jolt in the bottom of my stomach. Would it be possible? Could I leave crazy Samara behind?

"What about them? Do you like your life that much? We can have new lives. We can have better lives. Lives that we start on our own, lives we start from scratch where anything can happen. I'm done with my finals, and you can get your GED instead of finishing high school next year. Do you really want to go back? You hate your school. Come on."

I had never seen Tanya like this. She was sparkling. She looked happy, really happy, not just content that we had the house to ourselves for another weekend. Not just in bright colors. And she was right. What life were we leaving behind? I wanted to be happy the way Tanya was right then. But could I just leave?

"I need time. I need to think about it. When are you going?"

"I want to get out of here, but I can wait three days until you finish this year. There's a bus that night at seven. Meet me at the bus depot at 6:30 if you want to come. And if you don't, I'll write you when I get there and you can come visit or something.

"Come on, we don't need to rely on fate anymore. We can just make it happen. Make decisions, have convictions. Change everything or nothing about ourselves. It's up to us now. Let's just go!"

And with that she left, bounding off the porch and down the street. At the end of the block she turned around and called, "Come with me, Samara. Come with me."

"I don't know," I said, not nearly loud enough for her to hear. "I just don't know." Three days was hardly enough time. But, well, six weeks before, I had broken down in the grocery store begging my dad for a second chance. I could make my own second chance. I could make it happen for myself. Couldn't I?

chapter 16

The Heartbeat

Dee

J amie and I were sitting in my bedroom next to the door, listening to our parents talk. Jamie had told his parents what happened before they came over, and now we were sitting on the floor, leaning on the side of my desk with Jamie's arm around me, listening through a crack in the door to what our parents were saying about us.

"Look, the kids made a mistake," my mom was saying, "but they aren't bad kids. They're teenagers. And I know my daughter— she's trying to fix things."

"You have let our son run wild, and now look what's happened," his mom said, her voice breaking at the end.

"Honey, we don't know what happened," his father said.

"Of course we know what happened. First the drugs and the drinking. His schoolwork is falling. And now this. We know what happened. Can't she just…get it taken care of?"

"Get it *taken care of?*" I heard my mother's voice rise, and I could picture her eyes getting wider, even though I knew she wanted the exact same thing. She was fighting for me. And I hardly felt like I deserved it.

"She's just saying that this doesn't have to ruin anybody's life," said his dad. "There are ways to fix this. Whatever my wife says, we know that Jamie is a responsible young man. And he'll want to do the right thing."

"Oh, please," his mother said. "Have you met your son?"

"She doesn't mean it," I whispered to Jamie. "She's just upset. She doesn't know what she's saying."

"Yes, she does."

"I *know* our son," his dad said stiffly, "and I've talked to him. And I know that he's trying to do the right thing here."

"Well, he's obviously not ready to be a father," his mom said, "any more than your daughter is ready to be a mother." It sounded like she was spitting the words at my mom.

"My daughter didn't do anything wrong. Teenagers have sex. Are they in a bad situation? Yes. But if they think having this baby is the right thing to do, then I don't think it's up to us to make that decision for them."

"It *is* up to us. Look at what they've done. They're children," his mom said. "Jamie barely knows how to take care of himself, let alone a baby. He's completely irresponsible."

I couldn't take it anymore, hearing them talk about us like that. I might be sixteen, but I wasn't a child. And hearing his mother talk about Jamie like that…I got up and pulled away from Jamie's hand that was trying to hold me back. I walked into the kitchen, screaming, "Don't say that about him!"

"Excuse me?" said his mother.

"Do you even know your son? Did you see what was in the bag that he brought over here?"

"Dee, let it go," Jamie said quietly, walking into the kitchen behind me and grabbing lightly for my wrist.

"No. She can't talk about you like that." I pulled away from him and walked back into my room to pick up the bag Jamie had brought with him. I took the first jar out. "Prenatal vitamins…" the second jar, "folic acid…" two books, "a book about pregnancy, and one about giving birth…" the third jar, "iron." I turned toward him. "How do you even know I have low iron?"

I turned back to his mother, flipping open the book. "And here is the section of the book that he highlighted and flagged for me because he's already read it. It says that women who have at some point had low iron need to be especially careful about their iron levels during pregnancy.

"Don't say he doesn't care. That he's not smart enough, that he's not responsible. That's not fair. You obviously don't know your son."

Jamie stared at the floor, and his mom paused before asking, "You bought those things?" He nodded. His mom looked at him as though she was seeing him for the first time.

My mom put her arm out, and I walked over so that it would rest comfortably around my waist.

"This isn't a whim, is it?" she said, looking back and forth between me and Jamie. "You both understand what it is you're getting yourselves into?"

"Yes, Mom," I said, "we do."

❧

Two weeks later, Jamie and I sat in the waiting room before my first sonogram. My mom was going to try to get there right before the appointment started. We knew she was going to have to take a lot of time off work later in the pregnancy and after I had the baby, so she'd decided to try to build up some credit now when I was just about four months pregnant. I looked down at my stomach and was amazed I was showing so much already.

As we sat in the waiting room, I thought about all of the people who had sat there before us. The happy young couples, the men nervous and sweating, the women rosy cheeked and excited. The older couples almost tired of the whole experience, having their sixth child.

Maybe my mother had sat in a waiting room like this with my father before I was born. I wondered what they'd thought about, what they'd talked about, and I looked over at Jamie, who smiled at me encouragingly, squeezing my hand under his.

Finally, a nurse came out and brought me into a small room with a chair, a screen, a table where I sat, and a lot of equipment I didn't recognize. I looked at Jamie sitting in the chair next to me and took a deep breath to steady my emotions. I was lying on the table wishing my mom had made it in time for this. And even though we hadn't talked since before I'd taken the letter she had written to her mom, I wished Samara was there. Jamie reached over and took my hand again, stroking my hair with his other hand. The ultrasound technician came in.

All I could think about as she put the goo on my stomach was how cold it was and how much I wished my mom was there holding my hand instead of Jamie. But all of a sudden, I heard a soft thumping.

"Oh, my God, is that…?" I whispered.

The technician looked at me and smiled. "That's your baby." I felt Jamie squeeze my hand and lean over to get a closer look. "The baby looks healthy. This is the head, and the feet, see, over here?" She pointed at the screen. Jamie kissed the top of my head. "I'd like to see you again at the end of the second trimester. There's very little chance of anything going wrong at your age, but I'd just prefer to be on the safe side. Would you like me to print out the pictures for you?"

I nodded, unable to take my eyes off the screen. I tried to find the places she had pointed to again, but try as I might, I couldn't find the baby in the picture. I looked at Jamie, and he made a slight face and shrugged at me. At least it wasn't just me. The technician explained some of the things I needed to know about *taking care of my pregnant body* to me, and Jamie took me home.

The two of us sat on the couch staring at the picture, trying to remember what was the top and what was the bottom. He turned it over a couple of times, back and forth, upside down and right side up.

"Do you need anything?" Jamie asked. I looped my arm through his and put my head on his shoulder, still staring at the picture.

"No, just you. Look at this baby. Look at our baby."

We both looked back at the picture. "I have to admit something," he said after a minute and paused. "I don't see our baby. I don't see it. At all."

I laughed. "Okay, good. Me either. I just see a blob."

Jamie put his hand on my stomach and leaned down toward it. "Hi, Blobby. Can you hear me in there, little blob?" I laughed and heard the door open.

"Hi, sweetheart." My mom put a bag of groceries down and then nodded toward us. "Jamie." She looked at us. "What do you have there?"

"Ultrasound picture." I heard her walking over behind us.

"So that's my grandchild?"

"Yup," said Jamie. She kneeled down behind the couch and put a hand on my shoulder.

"At least, we think it is. I'm not sure which part is the baby…"

"So this is really happening." She paused, taking the picture. "See, there's the baby. The little peanut-sized thing. I'm sorry I missed the appointment. I couldn't get away."

"It's okay. Don't worry about it," I told her.

"Can you come talk to me in the kitchen, sweetheart?" I got up and followed her. "Listen, I'm still not sure that this is the right thing to do. I know that I've been behind you and I trust you and I hope you know that I will always support you, but you've got to understand that this is hard for me. But as my birthday present to you, I'm going to stop bringing this up and stop having this discussion with you."

I looked at her blankly for a moment and then realized that in the excitement of the baby and the first sonogram, I had completely forgotten it was my birthday. My birthday had always been really important to me, but that day, for the first time, my baby was more important than anything. My birthday included.

"Thank you, Mom," I said, falling into her arms.

Jamie walked in, saying, "Hey, do you two need help with—" But seeing us, he cut himself off and quietly left the kitchen.

∾

My next ultrasound was in April. I hadn't really been *hiding* the pregnancy at school, but I hadn't been showing it off either. As the weather got warmer, it was getting harder to wear clothes to cover it up. I would've looked silly in a sweatshirt with the temperature in the high 60s.

This time my mom was waiting at the doctor's office when Jamie and I arrived from school. She was holding my hand while I lay on the table, having stepped in front of Jamie to be closer to me. This time, I wasn't so surprised at how cold the goo was. We were all silent, listening to the heartbeat of my baby. The doctor turned around and smiled at me.

"Tell me," I said. "I want to know."

"Wait, are you sure?" Jamie asked me.

"Of course she's sure," my mom said. "We've talked about it. She and I have talked about it."

"Oh," he said, sounding defeated. "Uh, okay. Yeah, I guess we do want to know." I turned and mouthed, "Sorry," to him.

"You're going to have a boy. A healthy boy."

I could feel a smile taking over my entire face. I looked at my mother.

I turned toward Jamie. "We're going to have a baby boy together!"

He smiled and I could see that he was already tearing up a little bit. Then I turned toward my mom. "It's a boy. I'm going to have a boy!"

My mom nodded and squeezed my hand. "I heard," and she smiled and squeezed my hand again. "I'm going to have a grandson. Thank you."

On our way out of the doctor's office I whispered to myself, "I'm going to have a son."

∾

A week later, Jamie asked me to meet him at the mall at a children's clothing store after school. "I know it's not much," he said. "It's just a first step but I wanted to tell you I got a job here. I get a serious employee discount—30 percent—and the pay is $10 an hour. It's only going to be after school a few days a week until the summer, and then I can work full time. I know it's not a lot, but it's something. Something to start with. And we can get all the clothes we need really cheap."

He walked over behind the register and said, "Look, I already picked some stuff out, but if you don't like it, we don't have to buy it."

He pulled out a huge bag and put it on the counter, and an older woman walked by. I could tell she worked there because she was wearing the same blue shirt and dark blue pants Jamie was wearing. Her name tag read, "Denise."

"Hi, Jamie. Is this her?" He nodded.

"You are as beautiful as he said you were," Denise said to me. "Have fun, you two. He picked out some great stuff—seriously, great stuff. Show her the tiny overalls."

Jamie pulled out a series of onesies in different colors, little tiny jogging suits, and little tiny shoes and jackets, finally followed by a tiny pair of overalls.

"Wow," I said, "look how tiny he's going to be when he's born. Look how little these clothes are! He'll be so fragile. So little." I could feel myself tearing up, but I didn't know why. I tried to hide it but Jamie could tell.

"I know," he said, walking back around to put his arm around me.

"Ah, you're so wonderful." I hugged him back and gave him a soft kiss. Then the thought hit me. "Let's get ice cream!" I said. The craving hit all of a sudden.

"Okay. Sure, let me put this stuff away, and I'll let Denise know I'm going to take my ten."

I smiled at him. "Thank you, thank you for all of this."

"You don't have to thank me all the time, Dee. This isn't a favor I'm doing. He's my little boy too. My baby."

chapter 17

None of This Is Permanent

Samara

Tanya's parents told her that it was fine for her to move, to travel and try to find herself. But they wouldn't give her money to do it, so we agreed to stay for the summer and enjoy living off our parents' money for the last time, and then leave for Tucson at the end of the summer instead of right after the end of the school year. I hadn't talked to my dad about it. I wasn't sure how to tell him I was leaving.

A few days after Tanya's graduation, we were walking around in the rain. It was the warm spring-type rain that Tanya loved and that I hadn't enjoyed since I was little when my mom and I used to go for walks in it. Tanya jumped straight into every puddle even though she wasn't wearing boots. The two of us were already drenched but when she splashed a young couple, I dragged her away. They had been cuddled under an umbrella and looked less than thrilled at having been sprayed.

As we walked down the street, I noticed that Tanya was staring at me.

"What?" I asked.

"You just…don't take this the wrong way or anything, but you haven't looked this good in months."

"Are you kidding? I'm soaking wet and drippy and…gross."

Tanya grabbed my hand and pushed me in front of a store window. It took a minute for my eyes to adjust. I hadn't looked in a mirror for so long, and my reflection was…repulsive. I couldn't believe it was me; I couldn't believe I had let this happen to myself.

My hair looked shabby—it had been layered and it hadn't grown in well. My eyeliner was crooked—I had taken to applying it with the best of intentions, no mirror, and no way to check if it was drawn well. I looked at my eyes, momentarily surprised that they were mine and not Dee's. I had just assumed she would be there when I looked in the mirror again the first time. If I had thought about it, I would have known she couldn't just stand there and wait for me for seven months.

"Hey, don't be upset," Tanya said, putting an arm around me when she realized that the drops on my face weren't all rain. "You just need to clean up a little bit. Definitely get a haircut. Start doing your makeup with a mirror instead of at random. None of this is permanent."

I muttered a thanks and pulled away to walk home.

∾

I ended my moratorium on mirrors then. I couldn't believe I had let myself deteriorate so much in so little time. And all because I didn't want to talk to Dee. I had expected her to be waiting for me when I got back, and for some reason I had trouble understanding that she didn't want to talk to me.

I suppose in a way it was a relief. Talking to Dee had taken a lot out of me. Nothing was ever easy with her. It was the opposite of my conversations with Tanya. I could talk to her for hours about nothing. I had reached the point where being with Tanya was as easy as being alone. Dee had done that, somewhat. Tanya had said it months ago: it was because of her friends and because of Dee that we had met.

∾

We were at the beach, drip-drying after swimming, when two guys came up to us and asked us to come to a party with them that night.

"What are your names?" asked one of the guys.

Tanya rolled over toward me and propped herself up on her elbows. She looked gorgeous as always, wearing a pink-and-white-striped bikini top and blue board shorts. She looked back and forth between the two guys.

"I'm Jenny and this is Sandra," she said.

"And we're not interested," I said. "Thank you, though," and I smiled.

Tanya shot me a look and said, "We're not?"

I raised my eyebrows at her. "Ah," she said, "that's right. Sorry. Nice meeting you." They walked away, and then Tanya turned back to me and said, "You know what I'm thinking?"

"What?" I asked.

"Maybe when we're in Tucson we can try to find brothers to marry."

"Brothers?"

"Yeah," she said, "that way we'll be related. Wouldn't that be awesome?"

I smiled and lay back down again. What would it mean to be related to Tanya? What would it have meant to be related to Dee?

∾

I had put off making the decision about moving to Tucson for as long as possible, having convinced Tanya to stay home at least through the summer. I guess part of me hoped she would be willing to wait forever because I wasn't sure I was ready to leave. But I certainly wasn't ready to be here without Tanya.

At the end of August, Tanya finally had had enough. "Look, I'm leaving tomorrow. I can't put it off anymore. We've both been packed for weeks. I want you to come. But no matter what, I'm leaving for Tucson on the seven o'clock bus tomorrow night. I need to get out of here."

I was up the whole night trying to decide what to do. My life was revolving around Tanya at this point. I did almost nothing without her. What would I do here by myself? I opened the suitcase that had been packed and repacked a dozen times over the summer. Sitting on top was the stack of letters I had written to my mom. My mom was the only thing that I still felt connected to in this house, in this…life. I hadn't opened any more of the letters after the first, but I couldn't imagine leaving them here.

Or staying here with them.

∾

I met Tanya at the bus depot the next night. I felt like I was ready for a change. I didn't want to wait around all year and wonder what it would have been like if I had left. What it was like to raise chickens. To start over someplace where I didn't randomly run into people I knew in the grocery store.

I hadn't had the guts to tell my father, so I had left him a note. I made a few false starts, but eventually I wrote one I was happy with. I wasn't sure how to tell him I had up and left. I finally left this note, held down with my cell phone so that he would know he couldn't get in touch with me.

Dear Dad,

I know this is going to be hard to understand, but I decided to move. I can't stay here anymore. I need to get away from this life. I'm sorry I couldn't tell you this to your face. I think I was too scared. I'm going with Tanya to Tucson. We're taking a bus tonight. I'll come back to visit when I'm ready to. I'll call you when I get there. I'll wear a sweater.

I'm sorry to do this, but I need it. For me. To find myself, I guess. I'll get my GED. I'll get myself together. I need to get away from the memories I have here. From school, from you, from Mom. I need to be away from all of this, but I promise I'll try to come back one day. I'm not running away because I hate you or because I think you don't love me. I'm not running away from my life at all. I'm running toward a new life. A better life.

I hope you understand. I love you very, very much, and I'm not trying to hurt you. Please don't try to stop me. This is too important for that. I'll call you when I arrive. Just trust that I'm all right and I don't need anything. Thank you for everything, Dad. And thank you for understanding why I need this. I love you.

Samara

I added a picture of my mom and dad, the shirt I had been wearing the day my mom died, and the stationery I had had since I was seven to my suitcase. I looked around my room, unable to believe that this was the last time I would be leaving, the last time I would be turning the lights off.

࿇

When I arrived at the bus depot, Tanya's face broke into a huge cheery smile. "I just knew you would come," she said, jumping up to hug me.

"I'm so excited!" I said, though part of me still didn't believe this was going to happen. I knew that going to Tucson would be moving ahead instead of going backward. I felt like I had been living in the past my whole life, and I was ready to do something new. Something different.

When the bus pulled up, we looked at each other and giggled. It would take us three buses to get from home to Tucson, but with the first one, we would be on our way. When the doors opened, I put on my backpack and picked up my purse, and we both started rolling our humongous bags toward the bus.

We put our bags under the bus. It seemed like everyone at the bus depot was as excited as we were, and once our bags were stored, we both started to laugh as we got in line to have our tickets checked and get on the bus.

"Are you ready?" Tanya asked me.

Was I ready? Was I ready to leave it all behind, to leave without saying good-bye? Was I ready to give up my family, give up my friends, give everything up in hopes of something better? I looked at Tanya. Was I ready?

"Yeah," I said, smiling. "I'm ready."

"Then let's go. It's now or never."

Why was it now or never? Why couldn't it be after I graduated? Why couldn't it be next year or the year after? Why now or never? We got on the bus and found two seats together in the center of the bus. Tanya sat on the inside. Since she had a small pillow, she could lean against the window and I could sleep on her shoulder.

"I'm ready to be a chicken farmer!" Tanya said, and smiled.

"Yup," I said. Then we sat in silence, watching the scenery go from small houses to big buildings and then open highway until we passed into another state. Tanya had decided to change her socks every time we crossed a state line. I was amazed she had so many pairs of socks in her backpack.

"Kentucky!" she called, pulling out a pair of rainbow knee-highs. I was glad to be out of Ohio where it had been so dreary. It seemed like a cold drizzle outside, not the kind that was fun to run around in but the kind that leaves you chilled until you got home and take a warm shower.

Ohio had been all cornfields, and all the corn seemed to be an even height. Everything about the state was boring. I was excited to be somewhere new, but as it turned out, Kentucky was just the same.

I sat up and stared out the window. Tanya stirred and looked over at me.

"What's wrong?" she asked.

"It all looks the same. Is this whole country all exactly the same?"

"No, of course not," she said. "Look how much more yellow the corn is here. And look at how everyone is smiling. That's totally different than home. Don't you see?"

I guess I didn't. So I just curled up and put my head in Tanya's lap and fell asleep.

I woke up a little bit before our first transfer in Tennessee. I looked at Tanya, who was looking out the window, lost in thought. "Morning, sleepyhead," she said when I sat up and looked at her.

I smiled, but I was disappointed to find I was still on the bus. Not that I expected to be anywhere else; it's just that there isn't anything to do on a bus. There's nowhere to go. You're stuck there, and you can't get out. So I started to actually think about what we were going to do when we got to Tucson. We had printed out directions from the bus depot to a youth hostel and one cheap motel. Between us, we could afford to go about three weeks if neither of us found a job. We could find an apartment when at least one of us was working.

"So first we need to find jobs, then after that, I think we should rent an apartment," I said. She nodded. "Can you cook?" I asked her.

"A little. Can you?"

"As long as the food comes in a box. My mom died too young to teach me how."

"A boxed meal is my favorite kind," she said smiling.

"And tomorrow we can start trying to find jobs."

"Yeah. And if we can't raise chickens, we can milk cows or pick oranges or anything. Think of the possibilities."

"Yeah. Think of it." This had seemed so great because it was different, but sitting on the bus, I began to wonder why I was running off to become a farmer when I had never worked with my hands in my life.

And we thought about it as we sat in the bus depot in Tennessee, waiting for our transfer. It was a hot, sticky Southern night. Exactly the kind of weather we were trying to find. And as I sat on the bench sipping a Coke, I thought that if we got bored with Tucson, we could go to Southern California. We could do all sorts of things. I really could be anything I wanted to be.

"You hungry?" Tanya asked, returning from the gas-station store and plopping down on the bench next to me.

"A little," I said.

"Here." She pulled out a box and handed it to me. I turned the cookies over in my hands. *Lorna Doones.* I felt my heart skip a beat. What was I doing here? Was I running from the one person who really needed me?

I got up and muttered that I needed to go to the bathroom. Once there, I locked the door and looked in the grungy mirror. No Dee. Not that I should have expected to see her.

I counted how many months had passed since I last saw Dee and realized for the first time that she must have had the baby already. Was she okay? Was that why she hadn't come to the mirror? Had something happened to her while she was having the baby? Was she hurt?

I stared at the empty eyes in the mirror. Where was I? I was in a bus-station bathroom. I was going to a completely new place with a girl who, however much I loved her, I had met in rehab in a group therapy program. What was I doing?

Someone knocked on the door.

"Just a second," I called out.

"It's me. Are you okay?" Tanya called back.

I opened the door and she looked at me.

"What's wrong?"

I ran my hands through my hair. "Tanya, I'm sorry. I can't go to Tucson."

"What? Yes, you can. Remember? You're excited. You can't wait. Remember?"

I saw our bus pulling up. "I can't. I have to go home. I can't."

"You're just getting cold feet. Think of the chickens. Come on. It'll be fine." I could see a certain terror in her eyes that I wasn't able to place for a moment. And then I recognized it as the same fear I'd had for so long. The fear of being alone.

"Come on," she repeated.

"No. Just…Your bus is going to leave without you. I'm sorry." My voice was breaking. I hated when other people left me and I didn't want to hurt Tanya, but I knew I had so much else to do.

Going to Tucson was just not at the top of my list. "I can't. I have to get out of here."

"That's why we're going to Tucson. To get out of here. To get away. That's why we're going. Let's go. Come on, the bus is here."

"No. You go. Call me. I'll come visit. I promise. I just...I can't go. I can't run away. I have to deal with everything. I have to go back and face it. I have to go." *I have to find Dee,* I added silently.

"Last call, Houston," we heard over the loudspeaker. We both looked up, startled. Everyone around us had melted away in the hot summer night, and for a moment, only the two of us had existed in our argument. But the voice on the loudspeaker ended the lapse of time, putting us back with everyone else, reminding us that it was the middle of the night and we had to either stay or go—but deciding that later just wasn't an option.

"Come on. You made it this far. The bus is going to leave."

"Go. Take it. Maybe I'll come some day. I can't run away, though. I have to go back and fix what I messed up. I just...I have to go. Go. Get on the bus. Don't miss it for me."

Tanya looked at me silently. I could tell she knew I wasn't going to come. And I could see that she was angry at me for bailing out on her this late. When it was too late to find someone new. But she once again proved that she was a better person than me and leaned in to hug me, pulling me in hard.

"Good-bye, Samara," she said, and I could hear her voice starting to crack.

"Good-bye," I whispered back and pulled away to give her a kiss on the cheek. "I promise to come see you."

She grabbed her bag and walked toward the bus. On the first step, she turned around and waved, and then she vanished onto the bus.

I waited until the bus was out of sight to go and buy a ticket home. I wasn't going to figure out how to get through the solid mirror from here. I needed to go back and figure this out from my own room. From my own home.

I walked into the house early the next morning and found the note I had left on the floor. It was smudged, and I wondered if my dad had cried over it.

"Dad?" I called, but there was no answer. Where was he? I went into the bathroom to wash up. I splashed some water on my face and looked up. There was Dee.

"Samara!"

"Dee!"

"Wait there," she said.

chapter 18

They're Your Eyes

Dee

I t had gotten to the point where I just didn't care about school anymore. I was dealing with a pregnancy, trying to force my mother and Jamie to get along, and trying to prep for the baby. And the girl who had gotten me to this point was gone, missing. Not talking to me.

She'd stopped coming to the mirror after the night I took the letter she'd written to her mother. I thought I could help her. I thought I'd found a friend. But after all that time searching for an alternate universe, was either of us really any better off than we had been before that party?

∽

I was out looking for a crib with my mother after school one day. I don't think I'd realized how expensive having a baby would be before we started shopping.

We were looking around in the first store when a saleswoman came over with a briskly cheerful smile.

"That's a great crib. Very sturdy and safe. And isn't it just beautiful?"

It was beautiful. There were giraffes painted on the sides, and each had a different colored ribbon around its neck. The bars were unpainted wood, and there was a space on the bottom front to paint the baby's name. The crib came with a guarantee that there was no lead in the paint. It was perfect. I looked at my mother, but she pursed her lips and shook her head. "Excuse us for a moment," she said to the saleslady, who walked away immediately.

"What? It's perfect. Look at it."

"Yes, look at it," my mother said. "Look at the price tag. It's too much. The crib doesn't need to be so fancy."

That's when Jamie ran in. We were shopping in his mall, so he came over during his break.

"Sorry I'm late. What's going on? Hey, this one's nice," he said, pointing to the crib we had just been talking about.

"You know if you work in the mall, I can give you a 10 percent discount," the saleswoman said, indicating Jamie's uniform.

I looked back at my mom and raised my eyebrows. She just shook her head. We left the store after thanking the saleslady for her help. My mother and I wandered around in three more stores before we found a crib that was in our price range and we both liked and thought was safe. It was painted white wood. The side didn't come down, so we would have to reach over the top to get the baby out, but we thought that was better than him learning how to open the crib before he should be getting out by himself. The salesman gave Jamie a 10 percent mall-employee discount.

We knew assembling it would take us a few days, so we started that night. Jamie was coming over to help us finish it later in the evening after he got off work.

My mom and I were sitting in the middle of about five thousand parts that needed to be put together and staring at the instructions when I asked her, "What's the hardest thing about losing someone? Like a parent or a grandparent?"

I picked up a part that I didn't recognize and turned it in a few different directions to try to figure out what it was and how it was supposed to fit into another piece I was holding.

"Saying good-bye," she said without a pause. She was looking at the directions and trying to find a certain type of screwdriver.

"What if you don't say good-bye?"

"You'll never be able to move on. The person I was closest to when I was really little was my grandfather. When he died, I was too young to go to the funeral and I never really said good-bye to him. I think it took years for me to get over his death because of that."

I put my hand on my stomach.

"What?" she asked.

"The baby's kicking," I said, feeling my eyes get wide. Getting scared for no reason at all. My mother put a hand on my stomach and smiled.

"That's what's supposed to happen. It's okay, sweetheart."

I had made Jamie a copy of our keys, and he walked in and saw me holding my stomach. "What's the matter?" he asked, rushing over to me and crushing the section of crib my mom had spent an hour assembling.

"I'm fine," I said. "The baby's kicking."

"Oh," he said, leaning back and looking at my mom and an hour of work down the drain. "Sorry about that."

My mom sighed. "I'm going to get myself something to drink. Either of you want anything?" We both shook our heads.

"You know I don't think you should be doing this," Jamie was saying as my mom walked back in.

"She's pregnant, not an invalid," my mom said icily.

Jamie moved away from me and stood awkwardly near the couch. "Maybe I'd better go," he said.

I looked back and forth between him and my mother, trying to decide who was more upset and went with my mom. "Yeah, I think maybe that's a good idea."

That night in bed, I was thinking about what my mother had said and I decided that the best thing to do would be to have a second funeral for Samara's mother, a memorial service maybe, so Samara could say good-bye. Maybe I could still do something. Maybe I could still have that real friend that I thought I had found in Samara. Did it *have* to be too late?

She wouldn't just come because I told her to, I knew that. We hadn't spoken in months. *God*, I thought, *it was so much easier when we were kids and we could just share a two-part Popsicle. When ice cream was enough of an enticement to do anything. Mmmm…ice cream.* And with that I got up, finished off the pint of ice cream that was left in the freezer, and went back to bed.

❧

I decided to make a blanket for the baby. I bought some yarn and taught myself how to crochet from a video online. My mom insisted that I continue going to school, but that was easier said than done. The whole school stared at me, and as soon as I started showing, I became an instant pariah. With summer came an inability to hide the pregnancy at all. Jamie, on the other hand, was getting more and more popular. And didn't seem to see any reason to bring me with him. We just got in the habit of not really talking in school. It was fine; how much could I really ask of him?

I would sit in class, carefully crocheting the baby blanket in blues and greens. My teachers never called on me. I guess they accepted that I wasn't worrying about school anymore. Kelly approached me one day after class.

"How are you, uh, how are you doing? How are you feeling?"

"I'm fine. Thanks," I said.

"Do you want to hang out after school or something?"

I stared at Kelly. I didn't want to hang out after school. At least not with Kelly. It was just pity, I could tell. Nobody had talked to me in days. Kelly had stopped asking me to rework literary magazine pieces months earlier. It was like the world just melted away every time I walked into a room. The baby kicked, and my hand flew to my stomach.

"Are you okay?"

"I'm fine. He's just kicking."

Kelly stared at me. "Can I feel?"

I contemplated her. She was trying, I supposed. She was standing here talking to me, despite my status as the school leper. Girls I knew had had abortions, girls I knew had sex all the time turned and walked away when they saw me coming, whispering behind their hands.

That's the one, I'd hear. *Well, obviously. She's huge.* At least Kelly was making some kind of effort to talk to me, to maintain our friendship.

"Yeah, I guess so," I finally responded.

She put her hand on my stomach. "Wow. So it's a boy?"

I nodded and smiled. "Yup, my little boy."

Kelly paused but she looked like she wanted to say something.

"What?" I asked.

"I've just…I've never known someone who was pregnant before. I'm the youngest of my siblings and cousins and stuff so I've never, like, felt a baby kick before or anything. I don't know, I guess that sounds so stupid and immature to you…now that you're having your own baby."

"It doesn't sound stupid," I told her. "It's just the way it is."

Kelly smiled at me. "Well, see you around," and she hurried off down the hall.

"See you around," I said quietly to her back.

❧

School became a struggle. Well, just getting my shoes on in the morning became a struggle. I felt like I was snapping at Jamie and my mom constantly, even though I knew both of them were trying as hard as they could to help. Both of them were working full time, and I was sitting in front of the mirror all day, crocheting, watching my stomach grow, waiting for Samara, and eating ice cream.

I felt the pain in my back my mother told me to expect two weeks early, but once we'd passed eight months, my doctor had said not to worry. I called my mom and asked her to come home. She rushed home and brought me to the hospital. I asked her to call Jamie. She called him twice, but I guess he was at work or something and didn't get the message until I was well into labor pains.

My mom held my hand and kept telling me that the pain I was feeling was normal, that I shouldn't worry. I didn't find that particularly comforting. I really didn't care that other people often felt the same way. I hurt. Hurting is not something to just ignore. And as I was yelling that at her, Jamie ran in.

"Did I miss it? Did you have…" He clutched his side and took a few deep breaths and then ran forward. "Hey." He leaned down and kissed me. "You're amazing, Dee. I'm here. I'm sorry I'm late. I'm sorry it took me so long." He looked over at my mom who looked somewhat affronted by the fact that he had pushed her out of the way to get to me.

A doctor came in shortly after that. He looked at me, nodded, and said, "You're doing great. Now, after this one, I'm going to ask you to start to push. It's going to be a big strong breath and then push as hard as you can."

Anything, anything I could do to get this baby out of me was fine. My mother gave me her hand.

"As hard as you need," she said. "Okay, maybe not that hard." I tried to loosen my grip, but I felt the hand in mine switch. Jamie looked at my mom as he slipped his hand into mine, saying, "I can take it."

After one push I really would have been content to stop. It still hurt but not as much as pushing did. But the doctor kept saying, "Just one more big one," and I kept doing just one more big one and thinking about how lucky he was to be a man and to not have to give birth. I could have shot him, but just at that moment I heard crying and screaming. The doctor picked the baby up and showed him to me. I tried to appreciate how adorable he was, but all I could think was that he looked completely ugly. And slimy.

"Daddy, do you want to cut the cord?"

Jamie's eyes got wide, and he shook his head quickly back and forth. He looked over at my mom. Her eyes brimmed with tears and she nodded at the doctor. They took the baby away to clean him up, and I couldn't believe they were allowed to just take my baby away. Though when they brought him back pink and bald and cute and not slimy, I was glad they had cleaned him up. The nurse handed me the baby.

"He's beautiful," my mom said to me, wiping her eyes. "Just beautiful."

"Handsome," I corrected her. We were going to have to remember this was a boy in our family, not another girl.

He really was a handsome little boy. His head was so big and his body was so small that it seemed like he could have very well had no body at all. But his head was so cute that I preferred him this way. His body could grow big later. I kissed his forehead and Jamie ran his hand over the baby's head.

"Have you decided on a name?" the nurse asked, looking at me over the chart she was filling in.

"Samuel?" I asked, looking up at Jamie, who nodded at me as he stroked his son's little baby fingers and held his son's little baby hands. "His name is Samuel."

"That's a magnificent name, Lorna," my mother said. She had been there with me the whole time.

"Yeah," I said. "Well, he is magnificent."

∿

The ride home from the hospital was excruciating. Every bump and every turn brought more fear that the baby could get hurt. But we made it home fine.

Jamie met us at home with his parents. They were all waiting for us in the living room when we got back to the apartment.

I sat down next to Jamie and asked him, "Do you want to hold him?" He shook his head, but I pushed him, "Come on. He's your son. You should hold him."

"She's right," his father said. "I remember the first time I held you. This isn't an experience you want to miss."

"Just support the head," my mom said.

Jamie reached out and took Sammy from me. He looked so natural with a baby in his arms. Sammy was definitely Jamie's little boy.

I don't remember sleeping in the following three weeks. Sammy needed something all the time. But that was okay because I always wanted to give him something. I wanted to be with him all the time. I wanted to give him everything. I was so in love with him. I was so glad he was mine. My baby. My little boy.

Jamie came over as often as he could to stay up with Sammy so that I could sleep for an hour or two. Jamie's parents even came up a few times to hold and see their grandson. Having the baby seemed to have brought my mom and Jamie together, though it was pulling me apart from Jamie. We only saw each other for a few minutes at a time when he would come over to watch Sammy while I slept. We hardly got any time together.

❧

Sitting in front of the mirror all day waiting for Samara was out of the question. It felt like ages until Jamie and my mom had had overlapping days off. They decided to use their day off to give me a day off. I hadn't had more than a few hours to myself at a time, so I couldn't wait. They told me they would take Sammy out for a walk, go out for lunch together, then walk him around the park for an afternoon nap—he always slept best outside—and then come home.

The first thing I did was fall into bed because I was so tired. I hadn't realized it was possible to function on that little sleep. I woke up a few hours later and knew what the only other thing I wanted to do was. I took a long bath and then got dressed and sat in front of the mirror. I just had a feeling that Samara would show up that day. And I was right: it was only ten minutes until she did.

"Samara!"

"Dee!"

"Wait there," I told her. I ran back into my room and grabbed a picture of me, Jamie, and Sammy and the only picture of tiny little adorable Sammy where his eyes were open and he was almost smiling.

"Look! Look at my beautiful boys!"

Samara stared at the picture in the mirror. "Wow, he's gorgeous. Look at those eyes."

"They're yours," I told her. "They're your eyes."

"No," she said.

"Yes, they're your eyes." She smiled at me, and I saw her eyes, the same eyes my little baby had, beautiful and sparkling with tears. I wanted to hug her; I wanted her to hug me. "Can I?" I asked her.

"Please, yes, come through. Come please. Let me get a better look at that picture."

I stepped through the mirror, and Samara and I collapsed into each other's arms. We leaned back from each other only so that I could show her the picture of the baby I thought of as partially hers.

"So how are you? I haven't seen you in…I've lost count of time," I admitted. "In a long time."

"I'm okay," she said, "except I think I messed things up with my dad. I thought I was moving to Tucson with my friend Tanya and I left my dad a note, but at the last minute I changed my mind. He'd found the note already, though, and it's wet. I think he was crying. And he's gone."

I paused for a moment before asking her, "Do you have any idea where he went?"

"I think so," she said tentatively.

"I think I do too," I said.

"I think he went to see my mom. But I guess, well, I guess I'll just wait until he comes home."

"I think we should go," I told her. I knew this was my opportunity. I had been trying to figure out how to do this for months, and the opportunity had just fallen into my lap. If this worked in real life the way it had in my head, I would have the friend I thought I lost, my baby, and my boyfriend.

She furrowed her eyebrows but finally nodded her head. "I'm scared, though. Will you come with me?"

I nodded. I should have a couple of hours before Jamie and my mom got back with Sammy. As we walked, Samara turned to me. "What's his name?"

"Samuel."

"That's a nice name."

"I call him Sammy, though. Samuel is too big for him right now when he's so tiny."

"I'll help you out if you need me to. I can come baby-sit or something," she said.

I wasn't sure if I could trust her with my baby. We still had rebuilding to do. I knew that he was partially her baby, but I didn't want to commit to that so all I said was, "Thank you."

We walked along in silence until we came to the gates of a cemetery. She stood staring at the gate. "I can't do it. I can't do it, Dee." As she said it, a man approached us, offering us flowers, and I shook him off.

"Yes, you can," I told her. "It's time. You need to say good-bye. Even if this isn't where your dad is. You need to go in."

I looked at Samara, trying to read how she was feeling. I could usually tell. We had the same facial expressions. But I hadn't seen her in months. I was pretty sure I was doing the right thing, but she seemed so hesitant. I stood silently watching her.

She pushed the gate open and took a step in. I followed her, quietly keeping my distance, allowing her to lead the way. She walked and walked deeper into the cemetery until finally we found him. Found her. I stopped a few feet away and let Samara approach him. I was glad to do this with her, but a big part of me felt like I didn't belong here, felt like I was intruding on a personal moment. Like when I'd told her dad about her cutting.

"Hi, Dad."

"Samara," he said, looking up, his face tear-streaked, "you're here." He burst into tears again, and I looked down at the ground while they hugged each other. I wasn't sure what their relationship had been like the last few months, but if Samara had taken off without saying good-bye, they couldn't have been doing too well together.

I had gotten so distracted with my life, with Jamie and the baby, that it was hard for me to remember that Samara's life had been continuing as well.

"I'm here," she repeated back to her father. The sound of her voice reminded me where I was and why. I inched closer to her, wanting to be there and wanting to be invisible at the same time.

Tears were rolling down her cheeks as she looked down at the headstone. "I miss you so much, Mom. I'm so sorry, Dad. I'm sorry I left that note. I'm sorry I said I was running away. I shouldn't have done that. I won't do that."

She stepped away from him, glancing back toward me. It almost looked like seeing me gave her strength, and when she looked back at her dad, she said, "I'll stay and finish school. And we'll figure it out together. I'm not going anywhere."

I put my arm around her and whispered quietly into her ear, "Neither am I." She gave me a watery smile, and I tried to convey through the hand on her waist that she could trust me. That this kind of rift between the two of us wouldn't happen again. That I wouldn't let it. For the first time she looked relieved. Looked…calm? Or was I imagining it?

Her father stared back and forth between the two of us. "You know, you two kind of look alike."

Acknowledgments

First and foremost to Dan Ehrenhaft, who stepped into the roles of editor, agent, coach, boss, and personal cheerleader as necessary. Also to Leah, Kelly, and everyone at Sourcebooks for seeing me through from beginning to end. Joan and the entire 826NYC crew, who spend every day making the dreams of young writers come true and helping create dreams in kids who didn't know they were writers. And huge thanks to the other writers in my group from summer '05: Samantha, Kyisha, Dylan, and Will, who all gave me invaluable advice as I worked through the first draft of this book.

To all of the friends and family who put up with me through this whole process. Liz, who fielded the many questions that came from the Post-it outline of this book on our wall. Anna, who was constantly bucking me up, reminding me to be proud when I was feeling down and out. Both Kate and Catherine for immediately seeing the endpoint of all of this and reminding me of it when I lost that vision. All of Kane Street Synagogue, particularly Elizabeth, Emma, Eve, and Miriam for being the shoulders and the back pounders when I needed them. Ezra, for taking in stride so much more than I could have expected. To all of these people for teaching me what a best friend really means.

Aunt Liz, Uncle Barry, Aunt Joan, David, Jake, Ben, Nathan, Rob, and Ilana, you are the core on which I have built myself, the basis on which I have explored the world.

The many teachers of BHSEC who inspired me to write, create, and push myself to do better, including Dr. Ween, Dr. Clarke, Dr. Cordi, Mr. Peterson, Ms. Yaffee, Dr. Mazie, and Dr. Lerner.

The many other friends who supported me between there and here in a wide variety of ways: Adina, Rebecca, Connor, Ellen, Ben, Sarah, and Erica.

Finally, to the three people who lived and died with me with each version of this book, who saved copies on their hard drives without opening them, who inspired me: Mom, Dad, and Jesse. Without the late night phone calls and mid-afternoon emails, without the love and support you have given me, this simply would not have happened.

About the Author

Born and raised in Brooklyn, New York, Julia Mayer wrote the first version of *Eyes in the Mirror* as part of an eight-week program run by 826NYC during the summer between her sophomore and junior years at Bard High School Early College. She graduated from Boston University in 2009 with a double degree in philosophy and psychology. An avid swing dancer, she is also believed to be the only person to own a plastic hot dog signed by the 2009 Nathan's Hot Dog Eating Contest champion.

9 2 3 5 6 24 8 12 68 67

3 5 36 71 55 69 66 57

46 3 30 41 4 5 42 64 45

54 21 26 32 75 2 31 38

22 5 8 29 63 20 57 62 43

5 2 15 48 11 69 65 66 1 13

5 0